OPS' OBSESSION

SATAN'S RAIDERS MC
BOOK TWO

ELIZABETH KNOX

CONTENTS

Ops' Obsession

Editing: Kim Lubbers, Knox Publishing

Proofreading: Marybeth Higgins, Knox Publishing

Formatting: E.C. Land, Knox Publishing

Cover Designer: Clarise Tan, CT Cover Creations

Photographer: Sally Sparrow

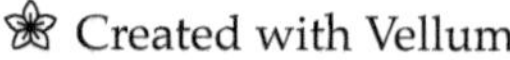 Created with Vellum

SATAN'S RAIDERS MC MEMBERS

Breaker — Prez

Chains — VP

Ops — Enforcer

Armor — Road Captain

Killer — Sgt. at Arms

Sarge — Full Patch

Brick — Full Patch

Ice — Full Patch

Agony — Prospect

Fury — Prospect

PROLOGUE

MABEL

Loud music pumps outside of the club as I wait for Puma and Celia to arrive at Silhouette. We have fun and love helping out local girls at the club. I haven't seen my friends in a few days because I've been working on my business, doing everything I can do to succeed. Not only because I want to prove to everyone that I have what it takes but also because I don't want to be dependent on my father for the rest of my life.

A heavy weight lifts off my shoulders when I hear the familiar laughter of my two girlfriends, "Hey, girls," I shout when I see the sexy bitches walking toward me. I don't know who came up with the saying that there's always one ugly girl in a crew of girlfriends because looking at the two of them, I know they're wrong. Both of them are fine as hell.

"Mabel, are you ready to party tonight?" Puma asks as she hugs me halfway and kisses both of my cheeks.

"Always. Hey, Celia, love." I kiss her cheeks, returning the affectionate gesture.

"Let's get inside. I'm ready for a drink." She blows out a sigh before she laughs, and she pulls us inside.

There is a bit of grumbling behind us as we're let straight into the club instead of having to wait in the line like the rest of the people trying to get in. Doing my best to keep the smugness off my face, I just smile politely at the guard who is holding the door for us. The bouncer lets us in. He's always going to let us in. This is the case with most of the establishments we decide to visit. Everyone knows who we are, more like who our fathers are. With one look at our faces, the bouncer waves us through the doors. We walk to the hostess desk, and she walks around the desk, hugging all of us.

"Just the three of you tonight?" Silva asks as she looks at her seating layout, probably trying to make sure that we've got the best seats in the house. I'd never cause too much fuss, but that's only because I've never had to. Those are just the perks that come along with living the life we live.

"Yes, we're ready to drink," I reply, smiling.

"Follow me, ladies." She winks and turns around, leading us through groups of people who are mingling around the edge of the VIP section. I feel eyes roaming over the three of us as we walk through them. Either they know who we are already, or they want to know who we are. Getting seated in this area means exactly what the name implies, that I'm a very important person.

The area is closed to the public unless you spend a lot of money, then you probably don't want to be so public. Bruno sees Silva coming and smiles when he sees Puma. He has a hard on for her, and I don't see the crush lessening anytime soon. Unfortunately, Puma's working on figuring things out for herself. She thinks her father is trying to get her into an arranged marriage, but she doesn't want that. I don't know who her father is thinking about springing Puma on, but if things are going how Puma thinks, I feel bad for whoever it is. Puma's not the one to be trifled with, and if she feels like her choices have been taken from her, she's going to let everyone know she's unhappy.

I'm sure Puma has tried to talk to her father about the possibility of a forced marriage, but our fathers think shit like that is normal. They believe that they know the right match for us just because of who they are. Those things are the ways of our fathers' lifestyle, but it doesn't mean that it's ours. I'm sure my own father has one for me, but he can fuck off with that bullshit.

"Ladies, Tamra is your server tonight. She will take your orders in a few moments," Silva says before walking off.

"Are we doing rum or Cristal tonight?" I ask as I look over the menu. I really do need to get a good drink in my system. I'm feeling the tension begin to rise back up. Relaxing is the only thing I want to do tonight.

"Both?" Celia giggles.

"We're going hard tonight?" Puma asks, raising her eyebrow at Celia before she turns to look at me.

"We're going to be eating too. So, Cristal before dinner and the rum after." I say as a way to appease both of them.

"Your logic sounds good to me," Puma comments, shrugging her shoulders and sticking her tongue out slightly in jest.

"Hello, Mabel, good you see you," Tamra sweetly states as she places napkins in the shape of cutout flowers on the table for our drinks.

"Glad it's you tonight, girl." I smile. Tamra knows us well. I really didn't want to have to explain to some new waitress everything I wanted.

"Do you want the normal?" She looks at us to confirm.

"Yes, on the food, no on the drinks. Water, of course, but a bottle of Cristal and rum, top shelf," Celia states, giving our order to Tamra.

She nods, not even bothering to write down what we want. Tamra never gets our order wrong. "I'll be right back with the bottle of Cristal and waters, and the appetizers will be out as soon as they are ready, then followed by your dinner."

"Perfect, Tamra, you're the best." Puma smiles while Celia and I nod, further validating what Puma had just said.

Just as soon as Tamra leaves, I heave out a deep breath. "Thank fuck, it's her tonight and not Tracey. I can't stand it when she's working up here. She acts like she's everyone's best friend, then stabs them in the back as soon as they turn around," I comment, slightly annoyed that Tracey even still works here.

"Tell me about it. She's probably the only one that I don't care for that works here. Most of the girls are chill and are working here because they need the income. I don't know about Tracey . . . There's something off about her," Celia replies.

"Yessss," Puma and I say at the same time, bursting into a fit of laughter.

Before we even have a chance to fully calm our laughter down, Tamra brings the drinks.

She places two buckets filled with ice and each of the bottles of alcohol in front of us, along with the cups of water. Finally, Tamra produces three empty champagne flutes, which she fills with the Cristal and hands to us.

"Thank you again." I nod to her before I pick up my flute and wait for Puma and Celia to do the same, "To friendships," I state as a toast.

"Friendships," echo Puma and Celia.

"I won't be able to hang out too much for the next coming weeks," Celia states as she swirls around her Cristal. "I have a business thing with my father." She isn't giving away any information, though if I could go off the way her expression just dropped, it doesn't seem like something she wants to do.

Puma asks, "What?"

"I can't say, just that it's working for my father. You know how private he is about his business. He would disown me if I said anything." Celia looks down at her glass.

"I hope whatever it is, you will be safe," I comment because I know her father is the leader of the 17. Whatever she's doing must be something to do within the cartel. I know better than to push for any more information. The last thing I want is for my friend to end up locked in an oil drum somewhere because she blabbed.

"Yes, I should be good. I hope it doesn't take too long because I'll miss my time with you both." She half frowns before she blows out a breath and smiles.

"We'll miss you too. You'll be able to talk on the phone, right?" Puma asks.

"Yes, sure. I should be able to. I'll answer if I can, but if not, leave a message, and I'll call you back when I can." She nods her head, taking a small sip of her drink.

"Enough of this sad shit. We have Cristal to drink and a whole night in front of us. Drink up!" I exclaim.

We drink up, and one of the girls, Sable, comes up to the table, asking if we want a private dance. I'm good, but I tell her to ask Puma and Celia just in case they do. They shake their heads no. We are having too much fun drinking, and we're getting ready to hit the dance floor. Just so she doesn't feel like she wasted her time, I give her five hundred for coming up to the table.

The night starts to speed by in a blur. The Cristal hit the spot with getting us loose. After our food, we began to drink rum, and that's when all the emotions started to flow.

"Bitches, I love you. I'm so glad you're in my life," Celia states as she holds her glass up for us to tap a toast. "You don't know how much I'm going to miss you."

"I think we have an idea, Celia. You've told us at least ten times tonight." I giggle, trying hard to keep focused on her.

"Let me tell you for the eleventh time, I'm going to miss you both," she nearly slurs.

"I think I need to cut you off. You're drunk," Puma states.

"I am not. I've just been drinking." She laughs and almost falls out of her seat.

I haven't seen her drink this much in a while. It's funny to see her falling all over the place, but deep inside my mind, I'm a little worried about her. Whatever she's doing for her father must be fucking with her head.

"I'll get us an Uber. I think it is the perfect time to call it a night."

I pull out my phone, load up the app, and schedule a ride.

"Our ride will be here in 10 minutes, which allows us to pay and freshen up before we go outside."

"Okay, thank you."

Tamra brings our bill, and we fight over who's paying for it, so we all pay for it, and Tamra can keep the extra as a tip. She has two kids she's putting through college, so she can use the money.

We freshen up and head outside. The Uber pulls up as we walk to the curb. We pile into the car, and the driver takes us to my house. Puma and I have to carry Celia inside once we are there. After getting upstairs to my apartment, we place Celia on the couch, and Puma and I fall into my bed. Sleep will come easy tonight.

CHAPTER ONE

OPS

One Month Later . . .

I close my eyes in an effort to calm myself down. The situation Breaker has us in fucking sucks. I don't know what the fuck his deal is, but I'm over him treating everyone, except a select few at the club, like total shit. What pisses me off the most is Breaker doesn't trust me, and he's made me a fucking prospect again. I've put my life on the line for this club time and time again, and I'll be damned if I continue to be a prospect. I've earned my place here, just like everyone else did too. None of us deserve this bullshit.

I look up, and Breaker's walking through the club-house. I can't bite my tongue any longer. It's time I said something to him.

"Hey, Prez," I say, trying to keep my cool.

"Ops, what's up?" he asks as he stops to chat with me.

"When am I going to get my patch back?" Breaker raises his brows, and I'm sure he can tell I don't give any fucks. I want what's rightfully mine back.

"You'll get it back once I figure out what's going on." Breaker begins to walk away from me, but I can't let him do that. This is bullshit, so I prepare to speak sternly to him.

"It's been over a fuckin' month, and I'm still a fuckin' prospect. That's fucked up." I grit my teeth, trying not to be too disrespectful, but he has to know this shit isn't right.

"You'll get it back once I figure out what's going on, and that's that. When I find out who popped my deal-ers, things can go back to their merry way around here." He sighs, obviously not liking that I'm sticking up for myself or my brothers here at the club.

I try not to roll my eyes like a bitch, but all of this is a load of bullshit. We have to walk on eggshells or what-ever, but he's keeping his new girlfriend around the club? It's fucked. It's totally fucked. None of us even know a damn thing about her except that her name is Cee. What kind of shit is that? This isn't shit I'm putting up with today.

"This is all bullshit, Breaker. Do you really believe people in this club would do this to you, to our brotherhood?" I flat-out ask.

"Yes," Breaker tells me, and there is not one ounce of hesitation in his voice. He looks over to his father, Ice. "How many times did your own people betray you back in the day?"

Without Ice even thinking, he says, "Many times. Most of these guys are in here for the brotherhood, but you get a few that can be bought for the right price. You think you might know a brother . . . but money changes even the best men," he states, then sips on his root beer.

Deep down, I understand why Breaker's being cautious about everything, but I think he's going about it the wrong way. He could've done something different, something that wouldn't have made everyone here feel like our Prez doesn't even trust us.

"I get all of this, but this isn't the way you should be going about it. Ripping away what we've worked hard for . . . it's not right. We all earned our patches and taking away what we spent so much time earning is just wrong, Breaker. Communication about what's been found and hasn't been found is lacking. You're leaving us out in the dark."

"Well, you can get the fuck out if you don't like the way things are going," he calmly states.

I was the enforcer before the shit hit the fan, and what he's doing . . . it pisses me off. I thought this situation would have been rectified before now, but it's dragging on. It's like whoever killed the dealers has an in somewhere, but it's not one of us. I *know* it's not one of us. They've been able to keep themselves hidden. Breaker can't see that. He automatically went to believing it was one of us instead of being someone who's been watching, listening, and even targeting us.

"I hope you're ready to watch your whole club walk away because you're being a paranoid idiot," I reply and walk out, my shoulders and neck tense with anger. I need to get the fuck out of here before I say something I'll regret and not be able to take back.

I glance at my phone and see the time. The Guatemalan woman, according to the bartender at Silhouette, will be at the strip club soon. I only know she's Guatemalan because the bartender knows I have a thing for her. The thought of her makes me smile as I walk outside, away from the bullshit at the club, and get on my bike. I head for Silhouette, waiting for the distraction that the place will give me. Maybe tonight I'll finally approach her, or maybe I'll just watch her from a distance like I always do.

The ride there helps me cool down, but Breaker needs to get his head out of his ass before the club completely falls apart. It's on that track now because I'm not the only one who isn't happy. I know there's some talk about people leaving, but I don't know if anyone will follow through. It *will* happen if we're left in limbo when it comes to our patches. I'm not the only one who's laid their life down for this club, only to have everything ripped off our cuts.

That was like taking an organ from my body. Those patches were who I was . . . what I am, who we all were. I feel like everything I've done has been a lie. Do I really want to start over with the same club where the president is saying he doesn't trust me? It's a kick in the nuts every time I walk in there, and I'm still a prospect.

I pull into the parking lot at Silhouette and park my bike. As I'm doing so, I push all the club bullshit to the back of my mind.

Silhouette is crowded tonight, and I go inside, finding my normal seat. I order a drink and glance around the place to see if she's already here and seated at a table with her friends. I can't find her. Since she's not here yet, I look back at the drink the bartender placed in front of me and take a sip. I turn my attention to the door, waiting for her to make her presence, knowing it'll be well worth the wait.

Twenty minutes later, she walks through the doors alone. Disappointment is evident on her face. Silva hugs her and then takes her to a table by the dance floor. I wonder where her friends are tonight, not that I care. This could be my sign that tonight is the night I should finally talk to her. I sit back and watch, knowing when and if I should make my move on her.

I turn back around to my drink.

"Ah, you saw her," the bartender nods in the direction of the Guatemalan woman I can't ever seem to keep my eyes off.

"I did. Do you know her name?" You think he would've told me her name ages ago, but I haven't been so lucky.

"Mabel. Her father has more money than he knows what to do with."

"Do you know what he does?" I ask, curiosity killing the cat.

"I don't, but she's loaded too." I don't care much about her money. All I'm interested in is finding out more about her.

"Got ya." I turn around and watch Mabel interact with the server.

She's gorgeous, and the dress she's wearing hangs on every curve. My finger itches to caress every inch of her body. The server brings a drink back to her table, and she downs it in no time. Then she gets up from her seat and walks out to the dance floor, dancing in the middle of the crowd. My cock hardens as I think about fucking her on the dance floor with everyone watching us. I close my eyes as I stretch my shoulders, giving myself a moment of relief.

The loud music pumps through the place, so loud you can't hear yourself think. I watch as men and women continue to buy her drinks and dance with her. They're touching her, and she doesn't care, especially since she's stuffing money in the club dancers' bras. Something inside of me doesn't like it. I want to yank her from the dance floor in a protective manner, to keep her close and flush against my chest.

A guy I've seen dancing tonight with a few of the women catches my attention. He's been all over the place, acting slimy. I watch him order a drink and then stop for a few moments at a table as she sits to take a break. Then he walks over to her, handing her a drink. He looks around and then focuses back on her as she takes a sip, and he smirks.

Fuck me. I get up from my seat and head straight to where she's sitting. I hope she's smart and listens, but all I know is that I don't like the feeling I have in the pit of my stomach.

CHAPTER TWO

MABEL

I'm so ready for a girls' night out with Puma and Celia. It feels like it's been so long since I've had a chance to really let loose with my friends. The Uber drops me off at the corner, and I wait impatiently for them to arrive. After standing there for a few seconds, getting antsier and antsier, I pull my phone from my pocket. I scroll through the message, only to notice Celia hasn't seen my text. That explains why she hasn't replied.

Puma has read it but hasn't replied. Bitch. I sent her another quick message, asking her if she was coming. After a moment, I see the little indicator letting me know that she reads the message but doesn't respond. Puma and Celia not showing or communicating with me is super weird. I'm not completely sure why, but I have a feeling it might have something to do with my father trying to set me up with Puma's brother, Silas. It is what it is, and I'm not changing who I am for anyone.

It's a business deal, and I don't want to be a transaction. I'm a human being, not a piece of property my father can sell to the highest bidder. On top of that, Silas isn't my type either. I would have to give up everything that I have and do to be the perfect trophy wife for him. If that's the life I wanted, I wouldn't have worked my ass off to get where I am now. If my father thinks I'm just going to waste all of these years of hard work because he feels like he knows what's best for me, he can kick rocks.

I don't need anyone to tell me what's best for me. Fuck that. I'm a businesswoman who can take care of herself. I don't need a man to keep me.

After waiting a few more seconds to see if the girls are going to show up, I decide to go inside the club. I barely smile at the bouncer as he lets me in without so much as checking my ID. The loud music washes over me, and I'm instantly in a better mood when I see Silva. Her hugs are the best.

"Just you tonight?" she asks as she releases me from a hug, a small hint of confusion in her voice.

"Just me." I shrug.

"Do you want to be close to the dance floor or in VIP?"

"Dance floor, please. I'm going to dance my ass off tonight." I let my head fall back and feel the music trying to push into my bones.

She laughs. "Follow me." She guides us through the throng of people and stops in front of a small table, feet from the dance floor.

"This is perfect. Thank you, Silva." I smile.

"You're welcome. If you need anything, don't hesitate to nod at me. I'll keep an eye out since you're alone tonight."

"You're amazing." I grab hold of her arm and squeeze it slightly before letting her go.

Silva is like an older sister, and we hit it off the first night I came. I feel safe being here without my friends because I know someone has my back. As I sit down, the server comes and asks me what I would like. It's not Tamra, but I guess I can't get everything I want. It doesn't really matter anyway. It's not like I have some exorbitant order, I just want to drink tonight, so I order a double of Zacapa rum and wait until she gets back.

"Double Zacapa. Is there anything else I can get you?" the server asks as she places my drink down in front of me.

"That's it for now. Thank you." I smile and hand her a couple hundred to pay for my drink and her tip.

"Thank you." She smiles.

I down the drink and let the warmth take over my body. After only a few moments, the familiar buzz of relaxation starts to pulse through my body. It's time to get on the dance floor and let loose.

I'm steady on my feet as I make my way toward the middle of the dance floor. I close my eyes briefly while the music takes over my body. I shake my body to the beat, really getting into the groove. I dance with whoever wants to because the dance floor is free for all. After a few dances, I feel like someone is watching me, not just the typical 'she's hot' glances I've been getting but something that breaks me out of my zen. I look around, but I don't recognize anyone or notice anyone looking my way.

The intoxicating beat pulls me back to the dance floor, and I continue to dance to the music. I'm already through my third song before the server brings me a drink. A drink I didn't order.

"Hey, girl. That guy bought you this drink, and there are a few more after this." The server giggles.

My eyes scan over her shoulder so I can try and pinpoint the person who bought it for me, but I don't put much effort into it, "Thank you. Make sure to let them know I said thank you." I smile at her. I sip the fruity drink, and before I can completely finish it, she brings me another drink and another. I wanted to drink tonight, so I guess tonight is my night.

After I finish the last drink, a random guy hands me a drink. I take it even though my inner alarm is blaring that I shouldn't be taking a drink from a stranger.

"Hey, I'm Nick," he says, getting close to me.

"I'm Mabel. Thanks for the drink."

"Nice to meet you, Mabel. You're welcome." He smiles widely.

I take a sip, and it tastes sour and sweet. It must be some kind of sweet and sour mix. I don't put the drink down as I resume dancing. This time I have a partner in Nick. His hands roam over my body, but nothing too aggressive. One song merges into another, and Nick dances even closer to me. My body begins to feel weird. Things are getting a bit fuzzy. I don't think I've drunk that much, but I could have since I've been here a couple hours now. I shake my head, trying to refocus my vision, but it doesn't help. Things are starting to blend together.

A guy in a leather jacket comes up. "Get lost, asshole," he says.

"I'm not going anywhere," Nick spits out.

The leather jacket dude gets aggravated by Nick, then tells him, "Get the fuck out of the club before I do something I won't be able to take back." I can almost feel the anger radiating off him, but I can barely turn to see what's going on.

I squeeze my eyes shut for a second, trying again to focus, "Did something happen?" I ask the guy in the leather jacket. There must be something going on if he's getting so aggressive.

The dude in leather responds, "You were drugged. I watched him put something in your drink when you were talking to the server with the long blonde hair. I'm sure it was X. Are you feeling, okay?" he asks.

"You're a fucking liar. Don't listen to him, babe. This guy is trying to get in your pants," Nick sneers.

A weird chill runs across my skin. I feel like my body's telling me to go into flight mode. Is that why I feel like I'm about to collapse at any moment? Did this bastard truly drug me? No longer feeling safe, I take a step toward the guy wearing leather, and Nick grabs me by the arm and yanks me back.

Leather dude instantly reacts, punching Nick in the face. I watch in shock as Nick falls to the floor. I stare for a few seconds until I realize the man knocked him out cold. It's impressive.

I normally don't need a man to save me, but something inside of me is telling me that I need to go with him. My mind is fuzzy, and I'm worried that if I try to go home on my own, I won't make it without someone else trying to take advantage of me. The sexy man in leather wraps his arm around me, takes me to my table to gather my things, and helps me as I waver a little bit as we walk out of the club.

He guides me into a 24-hour diner across the street and to a booth in the back of the place. I have to squint my eyes as we walk through the small place. The lights are bright and coming from the dark club, the brightness feels like knives in my eyes. Once we get to the back, we sit down, and I try again to get my body to return to normal.

"What can I get you, folks?" An older woman wearing a waitress uniform, a tight bun streaked with gray and worn sneakers, asks.

"Two glasses of water, two cheeseburgers with fries," the man in leather orders.

"Anything else?" She looks at me, making sure I don't want something different.

"That's it," I say, then do my best to smile at her. I'm sure it looks more like a grimace than anything.

The waitress must know I've had one too many drinks because she quickly brings water and crackers. I get that into my system, and I slowly start to feel more like myself. Our food comes, and I inhale my sandwich and fries like I'm starving. Maybe I was? Maybe that's why whatever was put in my drink affected me so bad. I didn't eat anything at the club. I look up and realize I'm eating with a complete stranger who saved me from God knows what back there and is sexier than sin.

"Feeling better?" he asks.

"Yes, I can think a little clearer now. Thank you for doing all of that. I'm Mabel, by the way." I offer him my hand.

"Good. I'm glad. Name's Ops. Nice to meet you, Mabel." He takes my hand, and jolts of electricity run through my body the moment our skin touches.

"I feel a bit happier, but I have a killer headache," I say, rubbing my temples.

His eyebrows furrow slightly at my statement, "Drink more water. It will help flush the drug from your body." He pushes the glass closer to me.

I finish my water, and I watch Ops through my eyelashes. Boy, he's nice to look at. My mind goes wild thinking about what he would be like in bed and warmth floods my center. Even after all that's happened to me tonight, just looking at this man is enough to make me feel the sharp bite of arousal.

"Can I take you someplace safe?" he asks once he finishes his meal.

"You mean somewhere safer than with you?" I answer instantly, raising an eyebrow in dare.

He cracks a smile, and fuck, I want to jump him. "Do you want me to take you home?" His eyes lock on me.

"Are you going to stay?" I don't miss a beat. Whatever was in my body must really be filtering out.

He shakes his head and gets up from the booth, and he looks down as he offers me his hand to get out of the booth. The current between us is driving me insane. Ops pays the bill, and we walk out together. The air between us crackles with lust, and as we walk by a dark alley, I pull him into it.

I push him against the building, kissing him, and his hands go into my hair, tangling strands in his fingers. He pulls my head back, exposing my neck, and he kisses from my lips to my neck to the top of my breasts. Ops pushes from the wall, removing his hands from my hair, and picks me up.

"Wrap your legs around my waist," Ops commands. The sound of his voice rumbles through his chest and vibrates straight into mine.

I pull my dress up and wrap my legs around him, and he pushes me against the building, using it to hold me up. He removes one of his hands from my ass and unfastens his pants, wiggling them down to release his dick.

"If you're wearing panties, you won't be after this," he says as he caresses my inner thigh to my bare slit. "That's a nice surprise." He chuckles as he inserts two fingers inside of me.

I moan out as he finger fucks me, and I tighten around his fingers as he brings me to the edge and stops.

"Ah, I was so close," I breathe out.

He doesn't say anything. I feel his thick tip at my entrance, and he slams into me.

"Oh—" He covers my mouth with his and silences my groan.

He doesn't let up, fucking me hard against the wall as the brick bites into my skin, causing the pain to mix with pleasure. My vision speckles behind my eyelids as my body feels like it's floating. With each thrust, waves crash through my body as I come on his dick. Ops releases my lips and pulls me tighter to his body. He grunts as his own release builds and his arms tighten around me.

"Fuck, I'm coming in your pussy," he grits out as he shoots his load inside of me. His head falls on my shoulder.

Ops kisses my neck as he catches his breath.

"Your place or mine," I say as he releases me. My legs wobble slightly as my body is still coming down from the intense high he just gave me. My insides hum with the slight discomfort that comes with being fucked hard and fast in an alley. I should feel ashamed of what I've just done, but for the life of me, I can't bring myself to regret it.

"Yours. I need the directions," he says as he zips his pants up and takes my hand as we walk back to the sidewalk. My eyes focus on the world around me and the feel of his hand against mine. That spark still floating between us, and suddenly, I'm more than just a little grateful that Puma and Celia decided to leave me on my own tonight.

CHAPTER THREE

OPS

I've had a lot of fast, quick sex in my day. Mostly with club whores or patch bunnies, but this chick has completely blown my mind. I've watched her at Silhouette for a while, and I make it a point to come to the club as much as I can because I love to see her. She's intrigued me, though. Over the last few weeks, I've done some serious digging into who she is. Finally, I found out her name, and it suits her—Mabel Castro.

Her father's Marcellus Castro. Everyone around here knows his name because his reputation is brutal. He's a large drug dealer and supplies the entire west coast with whatever choice of product they desire. No one is in the drug business and doesn't know who he is.

Marcellus is one of the top dogs, and he's the richest of the rich because of it.

I can't believe I just fucked her in the alley but being inside of her felt damn good. I've fucked a lot of bitches, too, but the others somehow don't compare to her.

"Your place or mine?" she asks while throwing her hair behind her shoulders.

Considering what happened earlier at the clubhouse, I know better than taking someone back to the club right now. I hope someday soon that'll change, but I can't be too sure.

"Yours," I say as I zip my pants up and grab her hand. She rattles off the address, and I realize it's right in the heart of downtown Los Angeles. We walk to my bike, and when we get there, I take off my cut. I help her into it, not wanting her to catch a chill while we're riding. I slip my leg over and get situated and help her get on without flashing everyone around us. Once she's settled behind me, her hands land on my thigh, but I force them around my waist and pull her against me. The heat is felt between us, so I start my bike and take off.

We weave through the streets of Los Angeles until she points to a parking garage near her address. I pull into the garage, and as I head further inside, Mabel points me in the direction she wants me to go. She directs me close to the elevator, so I park near it. The two of us get off my bike, and she takes my hand as we wait for the elevator. Neither of us speaks. We simply stand in each other's company, in the silence. Once the elevator doors open, we walk inside, and she taps on the number sixteen with the letter A next to it.

In no time, the elevator doors come to a halt, and Mabel enters a number on the keypad of the elevator. The door opens, and to my surprise, we don't walk out onto a floor. We walk into a studio apartment. Granted, this place is fancier than I'm used to. It's white and clean, with exposed brick. But why is Mabel Castro in a studio apartment? It might've cost a little over three-hundred-and-fifty thousand. Given who her father is, she should be able to afford whatever she wants, not a tiny place like this.

"You're living in a studio apartment in the heart of Los Angeles?" I question as I step further into her place. Her floors are concrete that's been dyed a deep amber color. The more I take in her place, the more I like it. Every wall in her apartment is white, and her furniture is a variety of cream and dark wood colors. She went for something very easy going here, and that contrasts well. She doesn't have a lot of space, but because of what she's done, you'd never know it.

"Yeah. It's small, but it's my little slice of home. All mine." She smiles as the elevator door closes behind us.

"Do you rent?" I ask.

"No, I bought it last year. It's the first thing I've ever bought by myself.. I'm really proud of it." Mabel admits, smiling lightly.

I give her a weird look. How is this possible?

She notices my expression, then explains, "My dad makes good money, and people accuse me of spending his money all the time. So, I went out on my own and made a name for myself. It showed them I could do anything I set my mind to." She smiles bigger than I've ever seen her do so before, and it lights up the whole room. We go over to the cream-colored couch and have a seat next to each other.

"What do you do for a living?" I relax back into the comfortable couch. The cushions are plush, and it sort of feels like it's molding around my body.

"I bought medical dispensaries around California, but mostly in Los Angeles. People love their marijuana."

"You must make good money, then?" I raise an eyebrow.

"I do." She shakes her head. "Great money, actually."

"Then why do you live in such a small studio like this?" I'm sure she could afford something much better than this.

Mabel laughs. "I'm hardly ever home, so it just makes sense. Why waste money on a massive place I'll never be?" She gets up from the couch and walks over to the freezer, opens the door, and pulls out a bottle. "It's Zacapa rum. Do you want some? It's a premium rum produced in Guatemala." She holds the bottle up for me to see.

"Sure, but you should drink some water." I don't know if the drug's still in her system, but better to be safe than sorry. I don't need her passing out on me or getting sick. If we can avoid it, we should.

"I'm fine. I'm safe in my own home," she says as she pulls two glasses out of the cabinet and sits them on the counter.

"Um, I'm a stranger, remember, and you could be in danger."

"If I were in danger, something would've happened a while ago." She pours me and her some rum, brings it over, then kicks her heels off and falls back on the couch beside me. "I mean, let's think about it. If you were malicious, you would've taken the opportunity that sleazeball back there started."

I give her a curt nod because she's right. If I was that type of shitbag, I would've done something already. All I want to do now is change the subject. "So, you know a lot about me, what about you? What do you do?" She sips on her rum.

I look at her and say, "I'm not sure." She looks at me like I'm a little bit crazy. "Things in my life are up in the air right now." I take a gulp ofthe amber liquid in the glass, letting it burn as it goes down my throat.

"I don't understand. What do you mean?"

"I was voted into my position because I did a good job at what I did. Something shady happened, and the man in charge removed all of us from our positions."

"That sounds a little extreme." I nod in agreement at her immediate understanding.

"I think it's bullshit myself, and I've told the boss that too. He isn't hearing any of it. That's why I wanted to come back here instead of my place. I needed some space, honestly."

"I see. How long have you been in your position?" Mabel questions, getting a bit more comfortable on the couch. She has her full attention on me now.

"I feel like it's been forever because it's all I know. I have years under my belt, that's for damn sure." It's the life I want to live until the day I die, but Breaker doing the shit he has only makes me doubt everything I thought I ever wanted.

"Have you thought about getting the same job somewhere else?" She takes a sip of her rum. If only it were that easy.

"I have. Several of my colleagues have thought about leaving. It's all about respect, and we don't feel like we are getting any right now."

"That has to be hard having everything in limbo. But, I have to ask you something . . . I see your vest. What are the Satan's Raiders?"

"Fuck yeah, it is. I like knowing everything that's going on and being left out in the dark is some bullshit. Some bullshit I don't need to be dealin' with, honestly. The Satan's Raiders is the motorcycle club I'm part of. Or rather, I was part of . . . I don't even know anymore. Before I had a title, I was one of the men who sat at the round table. Now I've been demoted, along with the rest of my brothers."

"Demoted to what exactly?" Mabel asks, furrowing her brows in the process.

"A prospect. So, it means we're at the bottom of the totem pole."

She's silent for a few moments. "How is that fair to any of you?"

"It isn't. That's why I'm so fuckin' pissed about it all. I've given my all to this club and to be demoted is a slap in the face."

"Not to mention extremely disrespectful, and not just to you, to all of you who have worked so hard." She yawns as she finishes speaking. That shit's contagious. I yawn, too, knowing I should leave, but I don't give a fuck. Being away from the club is what I need right now.

"I think it's a good idea to head to bed after we finish our drinks," Mabel suggests, and I agree with her. I'm beat myself.

"I agree. Don't forget to drink some water." I gently remind her, and she smiles lightly.

"I won't. I just don't want to be up and down peeing all night because I drank water before bed." She laughs.

"You won't bother me. I'll be sleeping on this couch."

"You will not. You can sleep in bed with me. It's the one luxury item in this place. Every other piece of furniture I tried to save some space on, but not this. My California king. I love my space when I sleep."

"You sure?" I question her, just verifying I'm not stepping on her toes.

"Yes, definitely. You wouldn't be able to get comfortable on the couch. You're too big." Mabel snickers at the end, and I now realize how small her couch is.

I nod, then down the rest of my drink, not paying attention to the burn. She finishes hers and takes both of our glasses into the kitchen. The open floor plan allows you to see everything that's going on in her place. The only area that's closed off from the living space is the bathroom.

"I'm going to get ready for bed," she says as she walks by the couch and into an area that's deemed her bedroom. She opens her dresser drawer and pulls out some clothes, then heads into the bathroom.

I lean my head on the back of the couch. What am I doing here? I have a feeling I'm going to get myself into trouble with her, but a little bit of trouble could be just what I need.

CHAPTER FOUR

MABEL

The very edges of sleep still cloud my mind as I curl up tighter and move my hand. It falls on something hard, and a spark of desire explodes in my body as I feel my fingers tracing over abs. I wake up in bed fully, opening my eyes, and I see next to me a shirtless Hercules. Ops climbed into bed after me, but I don't remember him pulling me into his body. He reminds me of the animated Disney movie I watched when I was a little girl, still learning English. Even at that young age, I remember thinking the main character was very handsome.

Ops has an arm around my back, so I'm able to give a little roll to get in a better position. I sneak out of bed, trying not to wake him up. A small ghost of a smile passes over my face as I look at him. Even sleeping, he's as sexy as they come. I let out a soft sigh and grab my phone. When I press the screen to see the time, I'm slightly amazed it's almost 9 in the morning. I don't usually sleep this late.

We arrived here a little after 2 a.m., so it's only right that I let him sleep a little while longer. As quietly as I can, I go into the bathroom to freshen up. Making sure to grab the robe that's on the back of the door. The robe is silky and short, and it's super luxurious, and I wear it when I'm at home.

After washing my face and taking care of my morning needs, my stomach lets me know that it's next on the list of needs that I have to take care of. As if to punctuate that point, my stomach growls loudly again. It would be embarrassing if Ops was awake.

I head into the kitchen and look in the fridge and cabinets, and decide to make scrambled eggs, beans, and fried plantains. It's a traditional Guatemalan breakfast, one I remember when I was back home in Uaxactún. Just thinking about it is enough to give me a warm feeling of nostalgia. Sometimes I miss home, even if there's so much I no longer remember.

My mother was born and raised there, and my father met her when he was on a trip back to Guatemala. She was in Livingston on vacation during the tourist season because she worked at a small hotel in a village close to the Mayan ruins. He was there for business on a ship, and they smashed uglies, resulting in me. He gave my mother his phone number in case he was ever in Livingston again, and the next time he called, she showed up pregnant. Talk about a surprise.

My parents were never together other than a few times during their life. They weren't in a relationship, and I grew up with my father. He moved me to America when I was eight, and I've lived in Los Angeles ever since. I guess I can't be too disappointed in how my childhood was with regard to my parents. At least they were smart enough to realize that just having a baby doesn't mean they have to be in a relationship. I'm glad I didn't have to deal with that drama.

As I continue to cook breakfast for both Ops and me, questions start to flood my brain. Starting with the fact that I have no idea if my father even likes beans. I don't know much about my father at all.

Even without him telling me, I know my father isn't the best man in the world. He has his demons that I know he sometimes struggles with, but I sense something bad. I'm twenty-seven, and he's never once told me what he does. Instead, he always tells me he's a consultant. I know what it means in the movies, and I'm damn certain my father isn't the loving, respectful man I want to believe he is.

The reason I moved out of his Beverly Hills home about two years ago is that he was trying to set me up with Puma's brother, Silas, in an arranged marriage. Of course, he wasn't happy about it, but I wasn't going to put up with it. Not when I was free to marry who I chose in this country. When he still tried to push the arranged marriage , I had to remind him of the year because it's not something that's done in this day and age. He laughed in my face and said in families like ours, it's done that way. I didn't understand what he meant, and he wouldn't explain it to me. He simply told me if I wanted to do things my way, then I could live on my own. That is what started my independence. I've seen my father on a couple of occasions, but nothing like how I used to.

Arms wrap around my body, and I jump as Ops tightens his hold on me. My heart stutters for a second, and I bite my tongue to keep from screaming out. I was focused on cooking and in my head about my father. I completely forgot that he was here. I understand how that is since I'm used to being here by myself.

"Goodness, you scared me." I breathe out.

He puts his lips on my neck. "Breakfast smells good." He moves my hair out of the way and kisses the other side of my neck. Even though his words are talking about food, his lips are talking about my body.

"It's finished," I tell him, and with a groan, he releases me. I laugh at his theatrics before I make quick work of making him a plate. "Have a seat on the island, and I'll be right there."

I dish up my plate, and I place it across from his. "Coffee, orange juice, or water?"

"Coffee, black, please," he responds.

"Okay. That I can do." I smile and turn around, walking to the coffee maker. All of this feels so very domestic, and I like it more than I care to admit.

I grab two coffee pods out of the drawer and make us both a cup. I get the half-and-half and sugar out because I like mine with milk and sugar. Once they are finished, I sit down across from him.

"Thank you, Mabel." He's already started eating by the time I get back from the coffee pot. He shovels the food into his mouth. A clear sign of someone enjoying their meal. "This is really good. You didn't have to go through all the trouble of making breakfast."

"It's nothing, and I was craving it. I miss home some-times." I shrug one shoulder and put a small amount of the soft eggs in my mouth. The spices and seasonings dance on my taste buds, and my mouth waters in preparation for my next bite.

He stops eating only for a second to ask, "When did you come here?"

"When I was eight, my mom died. My father brought me here, and I haven't been back since. I miss my culture sometimes, and I cook to connect myself to my mom and home. Of course, I love me a good pancake breakfast as much as the next person, but something about this meal brings back all the memories, you know?" I squint my eyes slightly, trying to gauge whether or not he's starting to feel overwhelmed by the topic of this conversation. It pleases me when he continues the conversation.

"That would be hard to cope with."

"It is, but I'm thankful for what I have here, so I try to look at it that way."

He smiles, and heat runs through my body. I really like this guy. I can't say there's anything overtly different about him besides how sexy he is, but there's some-thing that's drawing me to him. I have not ever genuinely been in love, so I don't know how it starts. But I do know I have some butterflies going on.

If there's one thing I've learned in life if you want something, you have to go for it.I settle the fluttering in my stomach for a second, "Would you like to go out again?" I blurt out.

"Yeah," he says and smiles brightly. "Would you like to see a movie this upcoming Friday?"

I return the smile just as brightly, "Yes, that sounds like fun."

He stops eating, stands, and gets his phone out of his pocket. After swiping the screen a few times, he hands the small device to me, "Put your number into my phone. I'll text you with my number."

"Okay." I take the phone and quickly enter in my information, then hand him back his phone. I'm tempted to do some picture peeping, but I control myself.

He looks down at it, swipes his finger across the screen a few more times, and says, "Sent."

A few moments later, my phone vibrates with a new text message. I opened the message, and it's a confirmation of our date on Friday. I smile.

"Got it, thanks." I put my phone down and get to finish eating. I'm trying not to obsess over what we're going to do before then since I don't want him to think I'm getting clingy.

"Want me to help with dishes?" he asks.

I'm slightly surprised he asks, not expecting all these good manners to come out of someone who looks like he's swimming in sin. "No, no. I got them. That's why I have a dishwasher." I hurry to take his plate before he can grab it, and he chuckles. He pulls the plate out of my hand anyway.

"I'm going to head out. I have some things I need to take care of." He stands up and puts his plate and cup in the sink.

I stand to do the same, but he takes the plate from me and places it on top of his. He pulls me into him, kissing me hard. I wrap my arms around his neck, deepening the kiss. I want this.

"I'll text you later," he says as he releases his hold on my body.

"Sounds good." I walk him to the door, opening it for him. He pecks me on the cheek and leaves.

I lock the door behind him and look at my phone. I have to fight myself not to text him right away. It's best to play these things smooth, even though I feel like a teenage schoolgirl on the inside. I scroll through my messages and realize that I have plans with Puma later. Exactly what I need. Something so I don't obsess over Ops too much. I head back to the kitchen and clean up from breakfast. Once that is all finished, I get ready to go out with Puma. I hope she feels like shopping today because I want to buy some sexy lingerie for my upcoming date with Ops. It's been a long time since I've had someone I wanted to impress.

CHAPTER FIVE

OPS

I put my kickstand down on my bike, parking it outside of the clubhouse, and I wish I didn't have to be here. I hate feeling this way, but it's the way it is these days. Shit at the club hasn't gotten any easier, and I don't know if it will. Spending time with Mabel's gotten my mind off this place and the problems here for a bit, but I know as soon as I walk through the door, I'll be in a foul mood. Everything that's going on here calls for it. I know, for a fact, that no one inside the club is going to be in a good mood. I try to think of something positive, but as I do, the door opens. Fury walks out, shaking his head. He doesn't even acknowledge me as he walks by, but I don't take it personally.

Fuck me. I want to turn around and ride out of here, back into Mabel's bed, but it's too late for me to make that choice. Instead, I walk through the clubhouse door. Tension hits me in the face as I walk into the club and look around. Most of the guys aren't talking, and I know it's because there's a rat in the club—everyone knows it. They're all looking at each other like they're suspects or possible rats, not trusting them with anything, not even their lives. It's a shame that things have come to this, but at the end of the day, this is Breaker's doing. It didn't have to be like this, but he deemed it so.

I shouldn't be here, or at least that's the feeling I have just standing in the club. It feels like I've been kicked in the gut, and I haven't even done anything wrong. We need to get down to the bottom of whatever's going on before it completely destroys the club. Unless it already has. The club could be too far gone at this point, but I'm not sure. Deep down, I have a feeling Breaker's going to feel like an ass once it's finally over because I still can't see one of the brothers being the person who turned their back on the club. It goes against every-thing we are.

I scan around the club and notice one person, in partic-ular, is missing—Breaker.

I know he's losing it. He's spiraling, and I've barely seen him at all lately when I've been here. Granted, I haven't been spending a lot of time here because of the toxic shit going on. Breaker feels like the only people he can trust are Ice—his father—and his new girlfriend, but what does he really know about her? I don't know, but I think it's all a bunch of shit.

I grab a drink and sit down at a table because I don't want to go up to my room yet. Once I do, I'm not coming back down unless I have to. It's almost like the club has become a prison. I can't speak for the other brothers, but I can't wait to get out of here because I don't know who's going to stab me in the back.

Chains comes up to the table I'm sitting at and sits across from me.

"What's up, brother?" I ask as he looks at me in a defeated manner. He has bags under his eyes that makes me know he hasn't gotten a good sleep in days.

"My mom's really sick, and it looks like she'll be passing away soon." He chokes up, shaking his head in the process like he can't believe it.

"Oh, damn man, I'm so sorry." That's gotta be rough.

"She's been fighting this for a long time. I hope she goes peacefully. That's all I ever wanted for her, for her not to suffer, you know?"

I nod, understanding what he means perfectly. "Are you gonna leave to say your final goodbyes?"

"No, she won't recognize me, and I don't wanna remember her like this. My mom actually died years ago. This is just her body finally going." He takes a deep breath and lets it out. "She has Alzheimer's, and when she sees me, she thinks I'm her father, and it just twists a blade in my gut. They didn't have the best of relationship, so it usually ends up with her telling me I'm a bastard and telling me she wishes I was dead. I know I don't have to explain what kind of total mind fuck that is." Fuck, I can't even imagine the shit that runs through his mind when he's seen her, and she's spoken to him like that.

"I understand your reasoning, brother. Let me get you a drink." I can't do much for Chains, but I can get him a drink to drown away his troubles for a little while.

He nods, and I get him a glass and bring the bottle of bourbon to our table. I pour him a glass and refresh mine.

"To your mother," I say as I hold my glass up.

"Thank you," he says as he holds his glass up and downs the liquid inside. "I appreciate you, brother. So many are keeping to themselves because of every-thing that's going on here, but you're one of the few I know I can trust. You're about as honest as they come."

"Thanks. That makes me feel a little bit better about being here. It feels like we are all against each other. There's no communication about what's going on, and I'm getting irritated with it all. I hope Breaker figures out this shit soon before there isn't a club to worry about."

"Amen, brother. That's how I feel. With this shit and my mom's health declining, I feel like I'm a damn mess."

"If you need anything, I'm here for you." It might not mean much, but I will always have my brothers' backs, regardless of what political shit is going on within the club.

"I appreciate it." He finishes his drink. "I'm gonna go outside and get some fresh air. I gotta make some calls, so all the arrangements are in order when she does pass. Thanks again."

"No thanks needed."

Chains gets up, and I pull my phone out of my pocket, looking to see if Mabel texted, and she hasn't. So, I shoot her a text, thanking her for this morning. As I rise from my seat, the energy in the room is still the same. I don't want to stick around, so I head upstairs to my room. I need a hot shower and to change into some fresh clothes.

I take off my cut and throw it on the chair in my room and pull some fresh clothes out of the dresser. The smell of Mabel lingers on my body, and as I take off the rest of my clothes, I get whiffs of her perfume in the air. My mind flashes to fucking her tight pussy in the alley. I can't wait to be buried inside her again.

Normally, I don't want to have a second go-round with anyone I've fucked, but Mabel's different. Maybe it's because I feel like she isn't with me because I'm in an MC. She's with me because of me, and right now, with allthis shit, I need that ego stroke, along with the dick stroke. It feels like every sort of relationship I've ever had with a woman has been a direct tie with me being part of the club, and it's a nice change.

I turn the shower on and let the water get hot, and I think about everything that's going on here and how Mabel was able to take me away from it. If it's okay with her, maybe we'll spend all day Saturday in bed, figuring out what each other likes. I chuckle to myself because I'm not this type of guy. Fuck 'em and leave 'em is my normal way of life, but here I am, trying to make plans with a chick.

Mabel isn't just a regular woman, though, and the more time I spend with her, the more I realize it. Ice has given me some words of wisdom in the past, and this feels like the ol' lady shit he always told me about. He said it would be different, that I'd know something deep in my bones. I know Mabel isn't like the rest. I'm not sure if she'll be my ol' lady, but I'm ready to find out.

The shower is at a comfortable temperature, and I step in, closing the curtain behind me. I let the water wash over my body and take the stress of being in the club-house with it down the drain. Something's going to have to change soon. We have to return to what we were before this all went down.

If we can get back there in the first place.

I don't know if we can anymore.

CHAPTER SIX

I wait for Puma to pull up outside of my building as I check my phone to see if Ops has texted me. I know it's silly to be so caught up on someone I just met, but I can't help myself. My face falls when I realize that there are no new text messages. As the realization that I've been thinking about him all day hits, I start to think maybe I'm more into him than he is to me. If that's the case, I need to hurry up and get over this crush. I'm not going to be made a fool of.

After taking a deep breath, I close the messenger app, but before I turn the screen off, the phone dings with a new text. It's him. All of the doubts I had seconds ago drift away. I feel giddy inside. What is this I'm feeling? I don't think I've ever felt so strongly about anyone so quickly. I think I have more than just a little crush on Ops, but I don't care. I quickly respond to his text just so he knows I'm thinking about him too before I put my phone in my purse. A moment later, I see Puma pull up to the curb.

She parks and waits for me as I get into her car.

"Hey, girl," I say as I get in.My voice is extra cheery, and her eyes squint at me for a second as if she's trying to figure out what's different about me. After a moment, she shakes her head and looks back toward the front window.

"Sorry about last night," she mumbles.

"It's okay. It all worked out. But while we are out trying dresses on, I want to go buy some sexy lingerie for next weekend," I tell Puma as she drives us to the boutique where bridesmaids' dresses are. I'm nearly bouncing in my seat with excitement.

Puma cuts her eyes to me for a second, "Why do you need lingerie, and what is going on next weekend?" she asks me before pulling away from the curb.

"Well, I decided that I was going to have fun in the club last night since I was stood up by my two best friends." I take a verbal jab at her and chuckle slightly when I see her grimace.

"Don't make me feel worse than I already do," she groans.

I suck in a sharp breath before I get on with my story, "Well, you're probably going to feel worse. I was dancing and having a good time, and this really cute guy came up to me. He bought me a drink, and I didn't think anything of it and drank some of it. Then a sexier than sin man dressed in all black and leather came to my rescue. The cute guy had drugged my drink, and the sexy man in leather punched him in the face, knocking him out, and he took me home. But before we went home, he made sure I ate something and was feeling better. Then I jumped him in the alley, and he fucked me thoroughly. I woke up next to him this morning . . . and we are going out on Friday." I finish the story with a high-pitched squeal.

"Holy shit, Mabel! You could have been raped. I am so, so sorry." Puma focuses on the fucked up part of the story. I guess I should pay more attention to that part, too, but I can't be too mad since all that happened and brought Ops to me at the same time.

"It all worked out. I'm okay, and Ops saved me. We really hit it off too. Like I'm able to talk to him and not think that he is using me for a business transaction with my dad or something." It's so rare that I find someone who either doesn't know who I am or doesn't know what my father can do for them. Usually, if I do find someone like that, it's only a matter of time before they figure everything out, and I become just another way for them to hit my father up for a favor.

"I'm glad it all worked out because that could have gone really bad. However, I'm sensing that you're more concerned with this Ops guy instead of the fact that you were almost raped." She chuckles slightly. "This is good news, Mabel. I'm happy that you're exploring some sort of romance with this guy. What does he do?"

"He's working with a shitty organization of some kind that isn't going so well right now. I plan on finding out more about it on Friday." I wave the question off as something not relevant. It is important, but after only a night with him, how much does she expect me to know.

"We'll get you some lingerie." She giggles. "I'm glad that we are in this wedding together and are both bridesmaids. I hate all this prep work, but at least I have you to do it with me."

"Me too. Although I have a feeling, these dresses are going to be traditional and ugly." I let my head fall back against the seat, and a flurry of hideous bridesmaids' gowns pass through my mind's eye.

"Oh, girl, don't say that. I'm sure that they will be fine." Puma does her best to quell my fears.

I humph before I turn to look out the window, "I don't know, I just have a feeling."

She parks the car in front of the boutique, and we get out and walk inside. I'm pretty sure we parked near a hydrant, but it's not like she's going to get a ticket. Even if some bozo patrol cop did give her one, she'd get it paid off immediately.

I entwine my arm with Puma as we walk up to the attendant, "Hello, we are here to try on dresses for the Gonzales/Ramras wedding," I inform the woman behind the counter.

"Oh, yes. They said to be expecting you today. Are both of you in the wedding?"

"Yes, I'm Mabel, and she's Puma."

"Okay, give me a moment, and I'll pull all the dresses Ms. Gonzales picked out for you." She rushes off into a different part of the shop.

I stare at the woman's back as she departs for a second longer before I say, "She said dresses, didn't she?" I look at Puma as I ask.

She shakes her head. "We are going to be here for a while." She giggles, and I join her.

"I knew this wasn't going to be easy."

"No, nothing is with her or her family," Puma sighs.

"Ladies, I'm ready for you," the shop worker calls. "I'm Ella, by the way, and I'll help you too. Let me lock the front door so we are not interrupted while you're trying on the dresses."

"Thank you, Ella," Puma says as we wait for her to show us the way.

"This way, please." She smiles as she walks past us and leads us down a hallway full of hanging dresses.

We arrive in an open room, and there are two daises in the room with mirrors around them, and the dresses are hanging on the racks on both sides of the room. Once I get a better look at them, I'm surprised at the quality and style. They are better than what I thought they would be, but there are at least ten of them to try on.

"Ms. Gonzales stated that she doesn't care which design you wear, but the color will all be the same. This way, we can pick the best dress for your body type. Do you have shapewear you will be wearing with the dress on?"

Puma and I look at each other and laugh.

"Sorry, that's funny. We're good."

We spend the next two hours trying on dresses and laughing because they are ill-fitting and look like we are five years old. Finally, we find dresses that make us look like we are adults.

"Oh, good. There doesn't need to be any major alterations," Ella says as I show off a form-fitting ankle-length dress.

"I like this one. I don't feel like a toddler in it."

"Girl. I like it too. What about this one? I'm comfortable in this one." The dress hugs Puma's curves and goes down below her knees.

"Yes, that's sexy on you. It doesn't look like a bridesmaid's dress."

"Good, that's kind of what I want." She smiles.

"That one fits you well too. I'm glad you came in, ladies. Neither of you needs major changes. The dresses will be ready for you to pick them up Friday before the wedding," she says. "When you take these dresses off, we will put your names on them, so no one takes them."

"Thank you," I say, then smile. She leaves the room, and we change back into our clothes.

"That took a lot longer than I expected." Puma looks down at her watch, and she bites her bottom lip for a second before she looks back up at me, "I have dinner plans with friends, and I'm late. I won't be able to take you back home."

It's not like her to leave me in the lurch, so I'm betting whatever plans she has are important. It's the only way she'd do something like this. "It's okay. I still want to go lingerie shopping, so I'll call a car. It's no biggie."

"I'm sorry," she says as she fixes her clothes and applies lipstick in the mirror.

"No worries." We grab our dresses and take them to Ella. "Thank you again for coming with me. I don't think I could have done this on my own."

Puma nods as we make our way up to where Ella is. We wave politely once she has our dresses in her hand.

"See you, ladies, soon."

We walk out of the boutique, and Puma is basically speed walking to her car now.

"I'll call you later," Puma says as she hugs me.

"Sounds good." I smile.

I walk down the street and call the car service, but they don't have anyone available right now, which I find odd, but whatever. There's always Uber. I get on the app, but no one can pick me up here, but if I walk a little way down Rodeo Drive, I can meet a driver.

Something doesn't feel right, there's a pit in my stomach, and I'm feeling a little sick as I walk down the sidewalk. I get that same feeling I had in the club when I thought someone was staring at me. It's like someone is following me. Maybe I should go back to the shop and wait until someone can pick me up from there? That's what I need to do.

I turn around, and three men in black shirts and slacks with black bandanas stand in front of me. This isn't good. Before I can move, I feel pressure up against my side as two of the men get on both sides of me. I know the object is a gun.

"Don't make a sound or struggle because I won't hesitate to kill you," the voice gruffs out.

Every bit of self-defense training floats out of my mind because all I can think to do is stand there and wait for the next instruction. Even if I could overpower one of them, there's no way I'd be able to get away from all three of them. There's only one option for me.

I can do what they say, or I can die . . . I'm not ready to die yet.

CHAPTER SEVEN

OPS

I'm chilling in my room, and my phone rings. Instantly, a smile tugs at my lips because the only person who would be calling me right now is Mabel. Or so I thought. My smile falls when I look at the name on the screen. It's not Mabel, but even so, I answer.

"This is Ops," I speak into the phone in a stoic tone.

"I need you to come down here and check on your guy. I believe he worked with you." I recognize this cat's voice on the other end of the line, but I can't place him. After a few moments, it finally begins to sink in. If I'm right, he's a cleaner, and I know better than to ask for a name. Cleaners are exactly what they sound like. They're people who clean up bodies.

"Fuck. Do you know who it is?" I question.

"I don't. But I brought the body into the warehouse behind where he was dealing. I don't need the cops sniffing around. They'll find more than they were bargaining for, and it'll fuck up a lot of my shit in the process." the man tells me.

"Send me the address, and I'll be there," I comment while a million things run through my mind.

"Will do." The call ends, and I'm certain I'll get a text message and then will never get another communication from this number again. They're always using burner phones. They use them a couple of times and then ditch them.

I check my phone, and he's sent me the address. I get off my bed, grab my cut from the chair, and then head out the door. I walk downstairs and through the clubhouse. No one is around, again, which is becoming a new normal. Not that it matters. They don't need to know where the fuck I'm going until I know for sure the dealer is ours. I'm just not liking the way things have been as of late. Truthfully, the more time that passes makes me feel like the club won't ever head back to normal. I head outside to my bike and get on, start it, and take off for the warehouse district twenty minutes from the clubhouse.

As I'm riding through Los Angeles, I open the throttle on the city roads. I don't give a fuck right now. I'm pissed off at the world while I ride my bike through the city to get to my destination.

I arrive at the warehouse, and I make sure I'm not walking into a trap. I pull my gun from my holster and survey my surroundings closely. There isn't a soul around, and I push the door open. Darkness surrounds me, forcing me to pull my phone out. I turn on the flashlight to see what's around me and shine the light around the open space. Ten feet in front of me lies a dark mound of blankets on the floor. I walk to the area sideways, not taking my eye off the door I came in through. In case it's an ambush, I want to be prepared. I make my way up to the blankets and kneel on the ground.

Using my gun, I move the blankets around, exposing a head, or rather what's left of a head. The guy was shot execution style, right through the forehead. He was a dealer. Good guy, working to put his kids through college so they wouldn't be like him and have to depend on the streets to pay his bills.

Motherfucker. Rage consumes me, and Breaker needs to get his head on straight and figure this shit out. It's not one of us. Most of us, if not all of us, were at the club or in our rooms. Breaker's the only one who knows where the dealers are working. I walk outside, putting my gun away, as I take a deep breath in an attempt to calm myself. This shit is just ridiculous, but ridiculous doesn't even begin to explain how shitty this is. I'm tired of the blame being pinned on us brothers when it's obviously none of us. I'm sick of the way things have been at the club since Breaker ripped our patches away. I'm done with all of it, honestly.

Even so, I need to do what I have to. I call to have the body moved, and I head back to the club after getting on my bike. The first light I come to is red, and I don't give a fuck. I turn because I don't want to stop. I want to get to the clubhouse as fast as I can. The longer I'm on the road, the more the fire inside of my mind is turning into a blazing inferno. It's time that Breaker and I get this shit settled. Depending on how it goes, I might be done with the club for good.

I pull up to the clubhouse, park my bike, and waste no time. As I walk through the doors, I realize it's eerily quiet. I go straight to Breaker's office and open the door without knocking. His girlfriend is giving him a blowjob and doesn't stop at the interruption.

"Who the fuck do you think you are?"

"Another dealer's been killed. Tell me what you're doing about it because what I see right now is you putting yourself before the club." He looks like I just punched him in the face, and honestly, I wish I would. Breaker deserves it and so much more because of how he's handling everything. I know it can't be easy to be the Prez in a situation like this, but he has to know there could be a better way.

"Stop, Cee. Give us some privacy. Go to my room. I'll be there in a few," he tells her.

She gets up off her knees, adjusting her top to cover her tits, and walks out of the room, wiping her mouth.

"So, where were you when the dealer was killed?" he sneers.

"I've been here all day. I was upstairs in my room when I got the call that the cleaner had found the dealer."

"Why didn't you say something when you left?" Breaker arches his brow, and I clench my jaw in response.

Is he seriously questioning me?

"Since I don't know where all the dealers are working, I didn't know for sure if he was our dealer or not. So, I went to check it out before reporting it. If he wasn't ours, I didn't want a false alarm."

"Sounds like some bullshit. Get the fuck out of here. No one in this fuckin' club can be trusted."

"How can you be so stupid to believe that Breaker? We have put in so much hard work and loyalty into this club, and you're pissing on it. You're pissing on all of us, our names, our commitments to the club, our fucking oaths. Is that what type of Prez you wanna be? The kind who doesn't give a fuck about his brothers, 'cause right now it's what you're doing. It's what you've been fuckin' doing."

"Get the fuck out now!

"Whatever, man." I leave his office, slamming the door behind me, and walk through the club, not stopping for anyone or anything. I see my bike when I walk out the door, and I get on it. There's only one place I want to be right now, so I call Mabel.

The phone rings once and goes to voicemail. So, I text her, telling her that I'll be stopping by and if she isn't going to be home, to let me know. I wait a few minutes, and I don't get a response. Maybe she's busy, but I'll still stop by.

I leave the club grounds and head onto the streets, and drive around a bit, clearing my mind. I don't want to bring all this stuff to Mabel's because she doesn't need to deal with the drama of the club, but I want to be inside of her. I want to forget about the fucking club. The club that's becoming the bane of my existence.

I'm tired of riding around aimlessly, and I head toward Mabel's place. Of course, I hit every single red light on the way there, making me even more excited to see her. I can't wait.

CHAPTER EIGHT

MABEL

Bile rises in my throat, and I have to force myself to swallow it back down. I don't need to be making a mess of myself right now. What I need to do is keep my head on straight. I can still feel the gun in my side, so I don't dare turn around, but I do try to mentally catalog anything around me that might be able to tell me who it is I'm dealing with. I'm not familiar with this area in town, so all I can do is focus on small landmarks. All of my efforts are moot when they turn me toward the van.

"What are you doing? I don't . . ."

"Stop fucking talking. When we want to hear from you, you'll know." One of the men behind me snaps at me. I close my mouth, but not before I hear a sad whimper die in my throat.

They push me into a van and put something over my head, tying my hands in front of me so I can't take off what feels like a pillowcase. They are speaking Spanish to each other like they don't think I can understand them. I don't tell them any different. I focus on the dialect and any accent that I can hear. To my surprise, they sound a lot like how my mother used to. Once I figure that out, I start to pay attention to what they are saying to each other. They have taken me because of my father, and I will be used to send a message to him. The van comes to a stop, and they push me out, and I fall hard to the ground. A sharp pain shoots through my knee, and I grind my teeth hard, trying to push through the ache.

"Make sure you get your phone out. The boss wants pictures of this," one of the men says as he laughs.

I try to stand, but I'm pushed down again. One of the men pulls the covering off my head, ripping my hair out with it. I reach up with my still tied hands, but they push them back down. One of the men in front of me grabs my chin and forces my face up so I'm looking at him.

"I thought you would put up more of a fight than you have, puta." I can't see his face, but I know he is grinning behind the bandana. His shifty eyes crinkle at the corners, and he stares into my face as if he's waiting for me to break down. I'm not going to give him the satisfaction. At least not yet.

"There are three of you to one of me, and you tied my hands. I'm not stupid." I spit back at him, trying to let him know that I'm not some timid mouse. I want him to know that this won't break me, at least not yet.

He punches me in the face before I can blink. Tears run down my cheeks as my face screams in pain. I should try to get out of here, but I'm afraid if I run, it will make whatever they are going to do to me worse.

"You sound stupid, puta." He picks me up and slams me to the ground, knocking the wind out of me.

I gasp for air as the other guy kicks me, not caring where his kicks land and the third guy stands back and takes pictures of what the two do to me. Fight or flight kicks in, and I attempt to fight back.

"You decided you've had enough? Well, it's nowhere near enough," he says, and he grabs me by the hair, then holds my arms down as his counterpart punches me in the face, so hard that I can feel my lips swelling as a coppery-tasting liquid fills my mouth. "Make sure you send those to her father." He laughs as I'm continuously assaulted.

My body is exhausted, and I want to give up. The pain takes over, and I'm on the edge of passing out. They continue to batter my body. My body is numb, and even things around me go dark.

"Mabel!" I hear someone yell. "Mabel!"

I try to move, but my hands are still tied together, so I try to talk, but my throat is dry, and nothing comes out. My tongue feels like sandpaper in my mouth, but I try to get enough saliva flowing to wet my lips. How long have I been out? Where are the men? What's going on?

I wait a few more seconds just to figure out if I'm just hallucinating or if I really did hear someone's voice.

My mouth starts to feel damp, and I'm able to stick my tongue out to lick my lips. The slight wetness feels so much better. The cuts on my lips burn, but at least I know I'm alive and probably not hallucinating.

That voice calls my name out again. " Here," I'm finally able to mumble out.

"Did you hear that?" a familiar voice asks someone he's with. "Mabel?"

"I'm here," I barely get out, this time a little louder.

"!Jue puta! She's in the dumpster," he yells.

I hear them get closer to me, then there's a light shining in my eyes.

"Oh, Mabel. We're going to get you out of here and get you taken care of," my dad's right-hand man, Miguel, says as he and another guy move the shit that's around me out of the way. I try to look up into their faces, but my head hurts so bad. I shut my eyes and just let them do what they will with me.

Tears stream down my face. Everything hurts. They pick me up, and it feels like knives piercing into my skin. I scream out in agony and try to move my arms but can't.

"Fuck, get a knife. Her wrists are being held together by a plastic tie," Miguel instructs him. A few minutes later, my arms are free, and I look down at the cuts caused by the nylon. I sigh heavily as I realize that's going to leave a mark.

I close my eyes and rest my head on Miguel's shoulder. "Mabel, we're taking you to your father's. It will be a few minutes, okay?"

I nod, not opening my eyes. Everything happens in a blur, but a few minutes later, I hear a car door open, and Miguel gets inside, not letting me go. The city streetlights pass by, flashing light into the dark vehicle. I'm fading in and out of consciousness, my head pounding with every bump we ride over. I don't know how much time has passed when we come to a stop.

The door opens, and Miguel gets out with me still in his arms. He has always been good to me. He even went as far as to tell me that he didn't approve of what my father was trying to do to me, but he said it was the nature of the business. What business I still don't know.

"Take her to her room," my father says as he meets us somewhere in the house. "I'll be up to talk to her once the doctor is finished with her." Miguel carries me up the stairs and quickly takes me to my room.

My mind vaguely takes a second to realize my father just said that there was a doctor in the house. How is that possible? I'm grateful but still confused.

"Doctor, she's been in and out since we found her," Miguel says as he places me on the bed.

A soft feminine voice speaks, and I open my eyes briefly, "Okay, I'll take her from here. Shut the door behind you, and I'll examine her."

"I'll be outside of the door, Mabel."

I look at him, but no words come out of my mouth.

"Hello, Mabel. I'm Doctor Sosa. I'm going to take a look at you, okay?"

I nod and let her examine me. It feels like she looks at me forever. She pulls out a portable X-Ray machine and runs it over my body, making sure that I don't have any broken bones. She helps me clean up. Luckily, I still have clothing here.

"I don't see anything that is broken, but you are going to feel it for a few days. You have a busted lip, swelling on the right side of your face from contusions, and cuts on your legs. Is your head hurting, or are you seeing double?"

"No," I answer quickly, but when she purses her lips and glares at me, I answer more honestly, "Okay, I feel like I got hit by a train. No double vision, though. Just a bad headache."

"Unfortunately, that is normal. If you notice after a day or so that the pain is getting worse, call me. Sometimes swelling hides fractures."

"Okay. I will."

"I'm going to talk to your father now. You can lie back down to rest. That's really what your body needs." She pats the one spot on my arm that doesn't have any bruises, but I still have to fight back a grimace.

"Thank you, doctor."

I lie down, hoping to just sleep for a bit. As I drift off, my bedroom door slams open.

"Who the fuck did this to you?" My father barks out, not even bothering to ask me how I am first.

My eyes snap open as I jolt up in bed, pain shooting throughout my body. "I have no idea."

"I want to know everything that happened," he seethes.

"I was walking from the boutique on Rodeo Drive, and these guys jumped me and beat me up." I give him all the details that I can remember.

"There has to be more to it!" He grows irritated with me. "I demand you to tell me more."

"I don't know what you want me to tell you." I fight with my memory trying to dig and find anything else that I can use to help. "They were Guatemalan because they were speaking our Spanish."

My father nods and crosses his arms over his chest, "That's the shit I need. Did they have any unique tattoos?

"I don't remember any, but they were wearing black shirts and bandanas." I shrug my shoulders and look away from him. I was the one beaten, and this is starting to feel more like an interrogation than anything else.

"That's it? That's all you can remember. You are fucking useless!"

"I wish I could've remembered something," I whisper. His treatment of me hits me hard, and I move off the bed and forcefully leave.

"Where the fuck do you think you're going?" He stops me, grabbing my arm.

"I'm going home where I can heal. I don't live here anymore, remember?" I jerk away from him as my body screams in agony every step of the way. My phone is broken, so I can't call for a ride. "Miguel, please take me home."

He looks at my father and nods at him. Miguel helps me downstairs and into the waiting SUV. I lay my head against the window. I wish my mom was alive. She would never treat me like this.

Miguel helps me get up to my place and tucks me into the couch.

"Thanks, Miguel."

"You're welcome, Mabel. I'm sorry all of this happened to you."

"Me too."

He leaves, shutting the door behind him as tears stream down my face. All of this is because of my father, and I still don't know what he does for a living. The tears don't let up as I cry myself to sleep, wishing things were different.

CHAPTER NINE

OPS

I pull into the parking garage and park where Mabel told me to park before. My bike fits in the space perfectly. I head into the elevator, ready with Mabel's passcode. I checked my phone before, and I still haven't heard from her, which I find kind of strange. The elevator ride feels agonizingly long, and finally, when I arrive at 16A, I input the security code. Mabel doesn't seem like the type of person to ghost me. So, I don't care about imposing on her.

"Who is it?" she hollers from the bathroom door. I head further into her studio apartment, and something just feels off. I imagined she would've been comfortable on the couch, not hiding in the bathroom.

"It's Ops."

"Go away."

What the fuck? No, absolutely not. There's something going on because she'd never just tell me to go away. I put my hand on the knob of the door and twist. The door opens because she didn't even bother to lock it. I slowly push it open, and Mabel whizzes by me, and all I see is a flash of darkness. She makes her way to the couch and covers herself with a blanket.

By the time I turn around, she's completely under a blanket on the couch. I get closer to her, and her breathing is ragged.

"Mabel, what's the matter?"

"Just go Ops. I don't want you to see me like this," Mabel mumbles lowly as if she's disappointed with herself.

"Mabel, I don't care what you look like. Now, take down that blanket." I urge her, and she gives in. As the blanket's lowered, it's obvious to me that she's been beaten. Her face is a mixture of fresh red marks, deep yellows, and even some hues of purple.

"What happened?"

"You don't want to know," she says as she tries to hide her face, but I pull the covers from her face, showing her that even though she's hurt, I still care for her.

"If it's your ex, I'll take care of him if you tell me to." I stand at the end of the couch, holding the end of her blanket.

"I don't have any fucking clue who did it," she cries, losing it. "All I want to do is feel normal."

I'm not going anywhere until she tells me to leave. I take a seat next to her on the couch and wrap an arm around her, pulling her close. I'll be here for her for however long she needs me to be.

"Okay, we'll figure that out later." I gently caress her hand. "What do you want for dinner?"

"I'm not hungry."

"You need to eat, so is it Mexican, Chinese, or pizza?"

She looks at me because I know she isn't used to a man standing up to her. Mabel better get used to it because I'm not going anywhere. I'll find out who did this to her and they'll regret touching her, but before I find them, I need to make sure she's taken care of.

"Chinese then. I want noodles and pork dumplings, please." She tries to get up.

"I'll call and have it delivered here."

I pull my phone out of my pocket and call the local restaurant, and they will be here with our food in thirty minutes.

"The food will be delivered soon. Do you want something to drink, or do you need anything?"

"Some water sounds good." She tries to get up.

"I'll get it for you. Rest. Your body needs it." I lean over, kissing her forehead, then get up to go to the kitchen and open the fridge to see if there is bottled water in there. I grab both of us a bottle and take it to her, opening it so she can take a drink.

"Thank you," she says, handing the bottle back to me. "You don't have to stay here with me. I can take care of myself," she mutters.

"I'm not going anywhere, Mabel. You were beaten up by someone you don't even know. What if they come back to finish what they started?"

"I don't think they will . . ."

"You don't know that for sure, and I'm not risking finding out. Right now, you're my priority. I'm going to make sure that you're taken care of until you're feeling better."

"Okay." She looks at me, more defeated than she was before.

"Mabel." She looks at me. "I'm not here to boss you around, I'm here because I care, and I want to make sure that you're taken care of. I know that you're more than capable of taking care of yourself, but I want to do this. I want to be here for you, okay?"

She nods her head.

"Good—" A buzzing sound coming from the elevator interrupts me. "Our food." I smile and walk over to the elevator doors, pressing the button for them to open. Mabel has a mechanism kind of like old apartments had back in the day, where you'd buzz them in to unlock the door. A young punk stands there with a couple bags of food.

"Chinese," he says, holding the bags open.

I pull out my wallet to give him a tip. All I have is a fifty, and I hand it to him. "Thanks."

"Whoa, dude. Thanks! Have a good night," he says as he steps back into the elevator.

Stepping back, I shut and lock the door before walking over to the couch and placing the bags of food on the table.

"Do you want a plate, or do you want to eat from the containers?"

"The containers are fine, but can you get me a fork, please? I don't think I can hold the chopsticks. The silverware is in the drawer to the right of the stove."

I head into the kitchen, open the drawer, and grab two forks out of there. Fuck chopsticks. I don't know how anyone can eat with those damn things. There are napkins on the counter, so I grab two of them and take them back into the living room. I place everything on the table and open the bags of food.

I thought she would've beat me to it, but she hasn't moved since I took the bottle of water from her. I'll take that as a hint that she's sore and doesn't want to move, so I open the containers of food and hand her one with a fork

"Are you going to be able to hold the container?"

"I don't know."

"I'll hold it, and you eat," I suggest, and immediately her expression shifts.

"No, I don't want you to not eat because of me." I appreciate that she wants me to eat, but I can wait fifteen minutes while she gets something in her stomach.

"I'll eat in a few minutes, but you're eating first." I'm firm with how I tell her, but not overly so.

"Thank you." She plunges the fork into the noodles and twists them around in the container, then puts it in her mouth. "Mmm."

I sit here, not saying a word because I know it's taking all the energy she has to feed herself. She's struggling, but I don't want to insult her further by trying to feed her. I offer her a container of dumplings.

"No, I'll eat those later if I get hungry. I'm full right now."

"Are you sure?"

"Yes, I'll probably eat more later, but I'm good right now. Although can I have my water?"

"Yes," I place the takeout container on the table and pick up the bottle of water from the table, taking the cap off before handing it to her.

She takes the bottle, softly putting it up to her swollen lips. I want to kiss her and tell her it'll be okay, but I don't want to hurt her. Mabel moves, attempting to set the bottle on the table, but she stops. "Ouch, this fucking sucks," she groans.

"I'm so sorry, baby. I wish I could take it all the way." I grab the bottle and put the cap back on, placing it on the table, then I gently pick her up and pull her into my lap. "What did your mom used to do for you when you hurt yourself when you were little?" I move her hair out of her face and tuck it behind her ear.

"She would sing "You Are My Sunshine" to me and make me bananas with sweet cream. It would always make me feel better. My mom always knew how to make me feel better. I haven't had a woman figure in my life besides my friends since she died. My father kept me home and didn't have me around any of his lady friends."

"What was it like growing up with him?"

"Very lonely. I have Puma and Celia now, but back then, it was just me trying to get used to living here in America without my mother."

"I couldn't imagine the struggle of having someone that was there for you, then someone not being there for you at all, or at least that's how I'm assuming your father was."

"Still is. He's not a good man. I feel it."

"What do you mean?"

"He was yelling at me, demanding I tell him who attacked me. When I couldn't come up with any information, he belittled me. That's why I came home. I knew I wouldn't get any rest because of him."

My body tenses. That motherfucker. He's worse than I thought he was.

"Don't worry about him right now. I got you." I lean down and kiss her cheek.

"Thank you, Ops." She tries to smile, but the swelling prevents her.

"Have you taken anything for the pain?"

"No, not yet."

"Let's get you to bed, and I'll get you some pain meds if you tell me where they are."

"Bathroom in the medicine cabinet."

I nod and hold her in my arms as I stand up from the couch and walk over to her bed, placing her on the edge. Turning the covers down, I pick her up and place her on her side of the bed and cover her up. I head into the bathroom, grab the ibuprofen from the cabinet and go into the kitchen to get a fresh bottle of water. I sit on the edge of the bed beside her, opening the bottle and the water, handing her both after she sits up in bed.

"Thank you. Are you staying the night?"

"Yes, I am. I'm going to make some calls, and then I'll be here."

"I appreciate you being here."

"I wouldn't want to be anywhere else, Mabel. Get some rest, okay."

"I'll try."

I lean down, gently kissing her on the lips. Anger fills my body, and I know I'll find who did this to her and make them pay.

CHAPTER TEN

MABEL

Six Days Later . . .

Ops hasn't left my side since he came to the apartment and found me beaten. My body still hurts, and I probably should have followed up with the doctor, but I didn't want to have to call my father. If I had gone to the hospital or seen a doctor outside of my father, there would have been so many extra questions. Questions that I didn't have the answers to.

Even after everything that happened, my father had yet to tell me what this might be about. He didn't even see it as necessary that I have any extra security. What if something like this happens again? I guess I'm not as important to him as I thought.

I hate that I have to see him today. Hopefully, I won't have to talk to him. I'd like to be as happy as I can be at the wedding. Everyone else doesn't need to be brought down because of the bullshit going on behind the scenes over here. It's supposed to be a joyous occasion, and I'm going to make sure that it is just that.

As I pick up a few extra things to pack away in my bag, my gaze drifts up to the mirror, and I spy Ops walking around the room. As the days go by, I find myself becoming more impressed by the man. Not only because he's so nice to look at, but because he's truly been a pillar of support when I didn't have anyone else.

I asked Ops to be my plus one at the wedding. He didn't hesitate to say yes. I've known men that would do anything to get out of going to a wedding with a woman they're dating, but Ops didn't seem upset by me asking at all. I'm kind of excited to see him in something other than black leather, although he looks damn good in it.

My eyes dart down to the soft sponge in my hand as a drop of concealer drops on my finger. It's taking me a little longer to contour today, but that's to be expected. I'm thankful for good makeup and Tylenol today. The swelling in my face has diminished a lot, but the bruises are lovely shades of purple and yellow.

They would match our bridesmaid's dresses, but I didn't want anyone to know what happened to me. I haven't told Puma what happened yet. I know she will be upset with me when I finally tell her since I kept it from her, but I don't want her to worry about me.

"Does this look okay?" Ops asks from my bedroom. I turn after one final swipe of makeup to look at him.

He's in khaki dress pants with a matching suit jacket and a white dress shirt. His dress shoes are dressy boots, but they work together. Who the fuck is this guy?

"Mhm. You look delicious." I smile and feel my upper thighs getting damp as I stare at him.

"Thank you." He chuckles. "I feel naked without my leather."

"I won't keep you at the wedding too long. It's a short wedding on the beach, and we can sneak out of the reception."

"It's okay. You do your thing. I'm just there to support you."

"Thank you. So, how does this monstrosity look on me."

"You look beautiful." He bites his lip for a second, probably to keep from laughing, "The color is interesting."

"Oh, it could have been worse, but this color of lavender is doable." I finish putting on my lipstick and give myself another look over. "I'm ready to go. I'll call for a car."

"I can drive us," he says before I can pull out my phone.

"You only have a bike?"

"No, I grabbed my truck and brought it here. I don't like being without it."

"Oh, that works then. Ready?"

He nods. I grab my purse and head to his truck.

We arrived at the venue thirty minutes later. The place was busy and crowded with all the people invited to the wedding. I swear Guatemalan weddings are just an excuse to get together and party. I think there are supposed to be over five hundred people here. I'm going to do my best to keep my beating a secret, but I'm sure there's going to be at least one person that will get a little too nosey. Even if Ops doesn't want to leave right away, I'll be more than happy for us to get lost and leave.

"I need to find out where I need to go. Please sit on the bride's side, and I'll find you after the wedding." I kiss him on the cheek. I don't want to cause too much of a scene because that shit gets back to my father.

"Will do, baby." He winks and walks off, taking in everything around him.

I spot Puma and walk toward her. Relief overtakes me when I see a friendly face. I was almost sure that my father was going to be the first person I saw when I got here.

"Who was that?" Puma looks past me over my shoulder. I'm sure it's at Ops. I'd be interested too.

"That's Ops," I say nonchalantly.

Her eyes jerk to mine, and they widen slightly, "You brought him?"

"Yes, I needed a plus one. Who did you bring?" I don't see why she's so surprised by this. It's not like I had any other suitors just hiding in the wings.

She bites her lip. "He's not here yet. I don't know if he's going to show."

"I'm sure he will. Let's go find out where we are supposed to be, so we can hurry up and get out of these dresses." I laugh, and she joins me.

The wedding was beautiful, and it lasted much longer than I wanted it to. All they had to do was say their vows and be finished, but no. they had to be extravagant. They had to have singers and recite their own vows. Then we had to take a million pictures. By the time it was over, I was ready for a drink. I look for Ops, and I see him leaning against the bar.

I walk toward him, and he sees me coming. He turns to the bartender and says something to him. When I arrive, he hands me what looks like a rum.

"You look thirsty," he says, taking a sip of his drink.

I issue him a wide smile, "Oh, very much so."

"So, are you going to introduce me?" Puma states from behind me. I turn and look at her, rolling my eyes playfully.

I pull her in front of me, "Ops, this is my friend, Puma. Puma, this is Ops."

He offers her his hand. "Nice to meet you, Puma."

With her most polite voice, she says, "Likewise. Do you mind if I steal Mabel for a few minutes?"

"Not at all. I'm going to step over here and check my phone." He points to a shaded area.

"Okay. I'll see you in a few," I tell him before he walks off.

Puma asks the bartender for a glass of wine. "Damn, girl. He's hot, and he seems nice," Puma says in a hushed voice over the top of her wine glass as if someone is going to overhear her talking.

"I know, and he's super sweet. Ops is like a teddy bear." Talking about him makes me realize how much I really like him. It scares me a little bit because I haven't been in a relationship where I liked a guy like this, but it doesn't outweigh my wanting to be with him. I'm ready to take this risk if it means I can keep feeling like this.

Puma sighs and tilts her head slightly. Her eyes are a little glassy, and if I didn't know any better, I'd think she's about to cry, "I'm really happy that you are giving him a chance."

"Me too."

Her eyebrows cinch in for a second before she looks back at me, "How do you think your father will react when he finds out?"

The giddy light feeling I had thinking about Ops vanishes, and I swirl my drink around in my cup, "I don't know, and I don't care. My father hasn't been a part of my life over the past couple of years, and I don't see that changing. He really doesn't have a say in who I'm dating."

Puma pushes a quick breath out of her nose and raises both her brows, "I hope so for your sake."

"Yeah, me too." I look out over the guests, trying to find any reason to change the subject, "So, did your date show?"

Puma's eyes quickly dart to the crowd, and a blush crawls up her perfectly made-up face. "He did. I'm going to sneak off with him since our duties are over." She gives me a hug and kisses my cheeks. "Love ya, Mabel. Be careful, okay?"

"Love you too. I will be." I squeeze her hand, and she walks off.

I watch her, trying to see if I can see who she's with, but she ducks out of my line of sight. Shaking my head, I turn to find Ops. He's watching me, and something flashes in his eyes. I smile. I think it's time for us to go back to my place.

He walks over to me. "Are you ready to go?"

"I am," I say as I take his elbow, and we walk out of the venue, weaving through the throngs of guests. A few people call out to me, trying to get my attention, but I'm not interested in talking right now. I'm only interested in one thing, and it involves the man whose hand I'm holding. We speed up when we get to the parking lot, and he kisses me deeply as he opens the truck door for me to get in.

The entire time we're driving home, all I do is stare at him. He reaches over a few times to touch me, but he doesn't push. Part of me knows he hasn't really tried to do anything over the past few days because of all the pain that I've been in. I tried to tell him a few times that I was fine, but he wasn't hearing it. It didn't help that every time I moved too fast, I cringed in pain.

Today, I'm not taking no for an answer. I'm too full of emotion and don't need to only have him hold me tonight. I need more.

We get up to the apartment, and the minute we do, he pulls the sports coat off and unbuttons the top button of his dress shirt.

"Ops . . ." I call out for him. He looks back at me but doesn't move any closer. "I'm going to need some help getting out of this dress."

He smirks and begins to walk in my direction, "I'm pretty sure I can help you with that."

I turn so he can grasp the zipper that's at the center of my back and pull it down. Before he can walk away, I twist around so I'm facing him. "My turn," I whisper and slowly undo the buttons of his shirt.

His eyes are heated, and even if he doesn't press the issue, I know he's as hot for me as I am for him right now. When I get to his pants, I don't stop. Instead, I pull off his belt and unbutton them.

When I snake my hand inside his boxers, he grabs hold of my wrist, "What you up to? You're still hurt."

"Ops, I promise you I'm not. The only part of me that hurts is my pussy. I miss you. I need you." I move my hand again, and he lets my wrist go.

His cock is warm and getting harder by the second. I grab hold of the thick shaft and slowly jerk him. His head falls back against his shoulders, and he lets out a tortured groan.

"Take me slowly. If you're worried about hurting me, take me slow. I just need to feel you inside of me, Ops, please." I pull my hand away from him and shrug out of my dress, letting him see me in nothing but the lingerie.

"Fuck . . ." he grabs the back of my neck and pulls me closer to him, "You will tell me the minute something is too much, you understand? Don't just try to push through it."

"I promise, I promise, please." I'm extra excited, my body gearing up for the release I haven't had in the last few days.

He dips his head and captures my lips with his. That zing of electricity I feel every time we touch buzzes over my skin. He runs his fingers along my body before he lifts me off the ground, forcing me to wrap my legs around his waist.

With sure even steps, he takes us back to the bedroom, and he lays me down on the bed.

He kicks off his boots and shoves his pants the rest of the way off, leaving himself naked in front of me. I want to taste him, but he's already on his knees before I can move. He pulls my panties down my legs so slowly that it feels like more punishment than pleasure. I know I asked him to go slow, but if he doesn't take me now, I might go out of my mind.

All thoughts of getting him to hurry snap out of my mind the second I feel that first swipe of his tongue along my slit.

"Oh . . . Ops," I moan, lay back, and let this man worship me in any way he wishes.

He rocks me slow all night until every last drop of my pleasure is wrung out of my body. When he finally lets himself come, we fall into an orgasm-induced slumber. I've never had anything like this before, but something about falling asleep in Ops arms feels so right.

CHAPTER ELEVEN

OPS

Sunlight cracks through the window, and I flutter my eyelids open, recalling every memory from last night. Mabel's lying beside me, her long hair spread out across her back. She's naked, the comforter coming up to her hipbones. All I can do is watch her body rise and fall with every peaceful breath she takes. I don't think I've ever seen anything more beautiful.

As I lay beside her, a heaviness weighs on my chest, and I can't say I've ever felt something like this before. In my past relationships, if that's what I can even call them, none of them felt like this. It's peaceful. I don't have to change who I am with Mabel, and that is a gift in itself. In the past, some women didn't like who I was with the club. Not all of them, but a few of them. The others only wanted to be with me because of my affiliation with the MC. I don't know what women see in men like us. They have to know we're dangerous, that our lives are dangerous, but they probably clearly see that being with us means they'll be protected. People within a club will do anything to protect their brothers and ol' lady.

I just wish Mabel could see what it's like to really be with a man like me. Sure, we've been together for a little bit now . . . but she hasn't gotten a real taste of the club lifestyle. Not in my opinion, at least.

My phone begins to buzz on Mabel's nightstand, so I reach over and grab it before it wakes her up. As my eyes land on the screen, I see its Armor. "Armor, it's a bit early for you to be calling," I say into the phone as I try to move as quietly as possible. I roll out of bed, plant my feet on the floor and walk into the kitchen. There isn't much space in here, but I want to give her some room. She was tossing and turning a bit in the night after our sexual escapades, so she needed the sleep.

"Yeah, it is, but if I'm callin' this damn early, then you know shit's hittin' the fan." Armor sounds aggravated, but there's something more underneath the surface.

"What's goin' on?" I question him, waiting for my mind to be blown. With shit the way it is at the club right now, I'm learning nothing's shocking me anymore.

Armor sighs heavily on the other end of the phone, and while I'm waiting for him to speak, I rummage around in Mabel's kitchen for her coffee grounds and coffee filters. The least I can do is have a fresh pot waiting for her when she wakes up, and it'll be nice for me to have a hot drink in the meantime.

Just as Armor begins to speak, I finally find everything I need. "I need you back at the club. We had a warehouse broken into last night, and shit isn't addin' up. It doesn't make sense, brother. Only a few of us knew about the location, and that was the place that was hit? It's fuckin' ridiculous."

"As much as I never wanted to believe it, we have a rat in the club. There's no denying it anymore," I admit, then fill up the coffee pot with fresh water. I pour it back into the reservoir while waiting for his input.

"I'd say. None of us can deny it anymore, and we're all lookin' at each other like we're suspects. I hate this shit, man."

I press the button to start the coffee pot, and soon enough, the brown liquid will be spilling into the bottom.

Armor isn't the only one who hates it. "I hate what the club is turning into because of this damn rat. We need to figure out who it is so we can deal with it. The sooner, the better."

"Yeah, I'm with you on that, brother. How long until you can get to the club?" Armor asks.

It'll take the coffee pot maybe ten minutes to finish, and I could probably get there in another fifteen after that. "I'll be there in half an hour."

"Good. Meet me at the club, and we'll ride out to the warehouse together," Armor suggests.

"Why don't we just meet at the warehouse? It'll save us both some time," I ask, and he grunts on the other end of the line.

"Sure, we can do that," Armor says, and then the two of us hang up our phones.

I wait for the coffee to finish brewing and make myself a quick cup. I can't take it on the road with me, so I practically chug the damn thing. I walk over to Mabel, who's still curled up in the comforter, and I kiss her forehead. She looks so peaceful, and it's nice. After everything she's been through, she deserves a bit of peace. She deserves rest-filled nights and all the happiness in the world. I may not have known her for very long, but I want to be the man who gives that to her.

I pull her name up on my phone and shoot her a quick text.

To: Mabel

I have to go handle some shit for the club. I didn't want to wake you. I'll text you a bit later. Sleep sweet.

I finish my cup of coffee, place the cup in the dishwasher, slide my cut on and grab my keys. Now I'm ready to leave, so I head down in the elevator and get to the parking garage in no time. As I mount my bike and start her up, I mull over who could be responsible for all of this. I go down the list of people who knew about the warehouse, and the list is long. Me, Armor, Breaker, Chains, and Killer know about it. We're all of the officers within the club.

I don't think Chains would ever go against the club. He's been here for almost as long as I have, practically as long as Breaker. But Armor doesn't seem like the kind of guy who would go against the club, either. This club is his entire life. Then I think about Killer and how he would never do this. The reality that I don't want any of my brothers to be responsible for this is right in my face. Trying to figure this out is going to be harder than I thought. At the end of the day, someone is responsible for everything that's been happening, and whoever it is will pay with their life. We've lost the lives of our people, our dealers . . . there isn't another option here. There isn't an ounce of mercy that'll be shown.

I get on the open road, and I'm at the warehouse within twenty-five minutes. It's right on the outside of the city and is tucked away in a barely used industrial park. A lot of the businesses who were here moved to a better area, which is why we chose to rent a place here. The club gets a lot of business through our bar, *The Clubhouse*, which is at the front of our actual club. We generate a good bit of income that way and launder money through the bar. We have to falsify our sales, but it's the best way to keep anyone who is sniffing around off our back.

I pull up next to the other bikes in front of the off-beige building. Once I've put my kickstand up, I dismount the bike and slide my keys into the pocket of my jeans. I head for the door and don't bother knocking as I walk inside. The warehouse is dimly lit, as usual, but it's lit enough that I can see tables flipped and boxes of liquor moved out of the way. We operate the warehouse under the guise of a merchandising building. We have our own brand of whiskey called Hell Riders Whiskey, and we have a farm out in Wyoming where we get our grain.

Armor's standing behind a broken box of whiskey, the liquor spread across the floor. Traces of white powder crosses the other part of the floor, a mere few feet away from the whiskey, and the cash boxes are broken with only a few dollars remaining.

"Fuckin' hell," I comment, completely blown away.

"Ops, we're gonna get to the bottom of this." Ice's voice comes from behind me, and the next thing I know, I'm hit with a forceful impact. I know I've just been hit, and my body wavers forward. Armor simply stares at me and shakes his head in disbelief. Meanwhile, another hit comes to the back of my head. Stars fill my vision, and the darkness soon consumes me.

CHAPTER TWELVE

MABEL

I pace back and forth, staring down at my phone. Ops never takes so long to answer me back.

I texted him a little while ago, but he hasn't replied yet. He did tell me that he'd need to go handle some business today, so I'm hoping this is the reason for the delay.

"Give him some room to breathe." I berate myself and toss my cell phone on the couch. I can't have my life be nothing but my time spent with Ops. I don't want to be one of those women that get so caught up in a man's life that I forget to have one of my own. Over the past few days, I've let a bit of the cleaning lapse in my place, so I can get some of that done before I even have a chance to gather my cleaning supplies, there's a knock at my door.

A flurry of reactions race through my mind. One, I'm hopeful that its Ops that's come over instead of texting me back. Two, I'm worried that it might be the same guys who kidnapped me before coming to finish the job. And finally three, I feel a bit of aggravation at whoever the hell it is for not fucking calling first.

I heave out a deep breath, trying to steady my nerves as I walk over to the door. There's a peephole, but I can't see anyone outside. Another knock on the door has my hair standing up on the back of my neck.

Ops wouldn't need to hide, so it must be someone I don't want to see. "Who is it?" I call out but don't dare open the door.

"It's your father." His deep voice calls back, and I jerk back at the sound. A knot forms in my stomach as I stand back on my tiptoes to look through the peephole again. This time my father shifts over, and I see that it's truly him.

My mind goes blank as I unlock the door and open it slightly. I haven't talked to my father since the day he basically told me I was useless because I got beat and didn't know who had done it. We aren't on the best of terms right now, so I'm not sure why he'd be at my door.

"Hey, Dad," I say but make no further move to do anything else.

"Mabel, how are you?" he asks. His voice is calm, with a twinge of concern laced through.

"I'm fine."

When I still don't open up the door, he shoves his hands in his pockets and exhales roughly, "Look, Mabel, I came here to tell you that I was sorry for the way things went down the other day. I really was a jerk about the entire thing. It's not your fault that you were hurt. I never wanted you to feel that way, even if my words made it seem different. I was just so upset about what had happened, and it seemed like I wasn't going to get any information from you about what was going on. It's my job to protect you, and I felt like a failure."

I'm stunned by the flood of words that come out of his mouth. I open my mouth to respond, but I still need a few minutes to get my thoughts under control. I open the door wider and beckon my father into my small home.

It's nothing like the roomy house he's used to, but it's mine. I don't need him to provide for me. I'm able to work for everything I've got on my own.

Once he's in and has taken a seat on the couch, I sit down in the lounge chair opposite him. I want to look at his face as he talks to me. If he's going to lie, I want him to do it by looking right into my eyes. I'm determined to find out some answers today. I never want to fight with my father, but that doesn't mean I won't do it.

"Dad, I'm grateful that you'd come all the way over here to apologize for what happened that night. You were so callous, but I can understand why you'd feel as you did." I wait for his reaction. He nods once, and I continue, "But I think I'm going to need some answers like why did this happen in the first place? What is it that you're involved in that caused those guys to come after me? Is it resolved? Do I need to watch my back at every turn?" My voice rises with each question, but my father doesn't bother to offer up any answers. He just sits back on the couch and stares at me.

"Mabel, if I thought any of those answers would be relevant at this time, I'd give them to you. But they're not." He shifts impatiently in his seat before crossing one of his legs over the knee of the other.

I throw my hands up and fall back against my seat, "Dad, if you didn't come here to tell me what's going on, I don't understand why you came all the way over here? You could have said you're sorry over the phone." I cross my hands over my chest and wait for him to explain his motives.

"Mabel, when are you going to marry Silas?"

The sound of the proverbial other shoe dropping booms through my skull. This is what he's here for? I can't fucking believe it. After all the shit that's going on right now, I barely know the man sitting across from me. Just because we have the same blood doesn't mean that my father is any less of a stranger. Now he really thinks that he can come in here and try to pressure me into marrying someone he deems fit simply because he's my father? He's not fit himself, so what the hell does that say about his choices.

I bite down on the inside of my cheek to keep myself from flying off the edge. It's remarkable just how pissed my father can get me, even though we barely say more than a few words to each other.

"Dad, I'm not going to marry Silas. We've already had this conversation."

He sucks his teeth and leans forward, pinning me to the love seat with his glare, "Mabel, don't be foolish. You can't stay running around the streets for the rest of your life just to spite me. I know what the hell I'm talking about. Silas is a good match for you."

"In what world, Dad, He and I have nothing in common. Sure, he could be a pretty good friend, but that doesn't mean that he's going to be able to handle being my husband. Not to mention the fact that I'm not attracted to him in the least."

My father's face turns up, and he shakes his head. "What does that have to do with anything that I'm telling you right now. I didn't ask if you thought he was cute. I asked you when you were going to marry him. When you were going to have someone take care of you better than you are capable of doing now on your own.

My blood boils at this remark, and I jump up to my feet, "Excuse me? Dad, I don't know where you've been the past few years, but in case you haven't noticed, I haven't needed anyone to take care of me. I work hard, and even though I'm not living in a million-dollar mansion, I do just fine on my own. I don't care what you say. I'm not going to let you or anyone else dictate how I live my life." He opens his mouth to say something more, but I put my hand up to stop him, "If that's all you came over here for, you are free to leave. I don't want to waste your time. I know you're a very busy man." I walk over to the door and open it for him, no longer looking at his face.

I'm so pissed. I feel like I might start crying at any second. How the hell could he do something like this? He's my damn father.

He grumbles something under his breath but doesn't bother to repeat it for me to hear. He walks out in a flurry without so much as a kiss goodbye, or an I hope you feel better. He's shown his true colors here tonight.

I slam the door hard when I hear his steps echoing down the hall. My chest is tight with the ball of emotion that has settled right there. I need someone to talk to. I go over and pick up the phone to call Ops, but I see he still hasn't had the chance to text me back. I don't want to annoy him, so I call my two best friends.

Having fathers like Puma, Celia, and I do make it, so our experiences are different from most. If there's anyone who would understand why I'm so upset about what my father is trying to do, it's them. Hell, Celia's father is trying to marry her off as well.

I shoot them both a text explaining that I need them to come over and that it's urgent. I don't bother to elaborate, and they don't pester me for more information. I know unless something life-threatening is happening to either one of them right now, they will be on their way to me. I crumble down on the couch and wait for them to show up.

Both of them are at my house within fifteen minutes, and when they get there, the first thing I do is break down.

"Oh, no! What happened?" Celia pushes into the house with Puma right on her tail, and they both wrap their arms around me, holding me up while I just let all the anger I have in my chest flow out of my body.

"Mabel, you have to tell us what's going on. I'm starting to freak out over here," Puma says, and I let them lead me back over to the couch, where they sit on either side of me.

"I'm sorry, it's okay. I'm okay," I tell them and do my best to get my breathing back under control. The tears were just a cathartic release, which was precisely what I needed at this point.

"Bullshit. You wouldn't be crying like this if you were okay," Celia says.

"I am now. It's just that my father was here, and he just makes me so fucking mad. I don't understand why he even had a child if he was set on treating me like this." I run a hand through my hair, and they both nod and stare at me intently.

"What happened?" Puma asks.

I proceed to tell them everything. If my father insists that what happened to me the other day is no longer relevant, then I didn't feel the need to keep it a secret any longer. I told them all about how I was kidnapped and beaten. I told them about how it was taped and sent to him as proof. I told them about his ongoing push to get me to agree to this arranged marriage. Getting everything off my chest felt so good. By the time I was at the end of my story, I was pretty much back to feeling like my regular self.

"When he came over here, I thought he was going to try to make amends. That's the only reason I let him into my house. My father doesn't want to make amends. He wants me to bend to his will. I'm not going to do that, ever!" I look between the two of them.

Puma's hands are roaming over my body, her eyes finally realizing that there are marks on my body from where I was beaten. "I can't believe you'd hide something like this from me! Why didn't you tell me when we were at the wedding? I hate that you had to go through all that by yourself."

I smile softly, "Well, I wasn't alone. Ops stayed with me the whole time. I thought for sure that he was going to fly off the handle when he walked in and saw me all beat up like that, but he kept his cool and just took care of me."

Puma releases a cliché, "Aww."

I can feel myself start to blush. I look at Celia, but she's not really paying attention. Instead, she seems like she's in deep thought. I hope I didn't scare her into thinking something like this could happen to her. I wouldn't wish what happened to me on anyone.

"You okay?" I ask her, and she snaps out of her daze and gives me a tight smile. I leave her be and continue talking things over with Puma. Maybe Celia had a bad day. Either way, I'm just happy they are both here with me now.

CHAPTER THIRTEEN

OPS

My head pounds as I finally come to, then it hits me—
Ice being in a place he shouldn't even have known
about, being hit in the back of the head, Armor's
words, falling forward. I have no doubt in my mind
they think I'm the fucking rat. Me . . . of all people . . .
is who they're certain is the one betraying the club. I
don't know whether to laugh or be pissed.

"Is this some sick, twisted joke?" I seethe, thrashing my
arms that are tied behind me. I glance down, seeing
they've got me tied to an old wooden chair.

"I wish it was," Breaker says in the angriest voice I've
ever heard.

Ice steps under the light, and I see part of Armor's face off to the left. "You're a weak son of a bitch for doin' that to me. You know it, too," I hiss at Ice. They could've done this the easy way, not like some back-woods shady shit.

"I did what needed to be done, son. Deep down, you know that. Deep down, you know you would've run if given the opportunity. You didn't want us to catch you, but we have, so now's the time to make shit right." Ice goes on. To say I'm in shock would be an under-statement.

"Now's the time to make things right, brother," Armor finally speaks up, stepping further into the light.

"Make things right? You've gotta be fuckin' kiddin' me right now! I haven't done shit to this club!" I snarl at the three of them, and Breaker cackles, shaking his head while doing so.

"You really think we don't know what you've been doin'?" Breaker approaches me, picks up a piece of rebar from off the ground, and slams it against the side of my face. A loud *pop* floods through me the second the metal hits me.

I spit blood out onto the concrete floor and glare up at the man I formerly followed. I don't know if I'll ever be able to follow Breaker again. Not after a betrayal like this. "And what exactly is that, huh?" I thrash in the chair, needing my fury to be evident.

Armor shakes his head in disapproval, and Ice stares at me the same way he'd look at any 'traitor'.

"You've been shackin' up with a drug princess, Ops. We all know it. Kinda convenient that all this shit starts happenin' right around the time you start hookin' up with Mabel Castro." Breaker's nostrils flare with every word, and I'm caught in a bit of disbelief.

Sure, I knew being with Mabel could be an issue . . . her father's our direct competition, but she has no part of his world. "She isn't part of the drugs. She's made a name for herself and distanced herself from that shit."

"She makes her money from owning medical marijuana facilities. I'd hardly say she's distanced herself from that shit," Armor points out. I know he's here because he believes I'm the rat too, but he's the only one treating me like I'm somewhat human. Meanwhile, Ice and Breaker are ready to put a bullet in me and dispose of my body. Armor could be my only chance to get out of this alive.

"She doesn't fuck with her father's business. I'm tellin' you that here and now. Mabel isn't like that." I raise my voice and glare at every man in the room.

"How long have you been with her, Ops?" Ice questions, coming closer to me. He grabs the rebar from Breaker and slams it down on my leg. The breath in my lungs leaves me, and I struggle to inhale again as pain radiates down my leg.

"Stop bein' a little bitch, Ice. I'm not hidin' shit from any of you. I've been with her for a few weeks, and I don't talk about club shit with her. She's not the first woman I've been with since bein' in the club. I know how this shit works. I know not to open my fuckin' mouth."

Mabel's the first woman I've been with that's had drug affiliations, but I've never told any other women about that type of shit. Unless you're my ol' lady, you don't know anything. Mabel isn't my ol' lady—yet. I could see her being by my side for a very long time, though. She's the only woman I've ever felt like could be my ride or die.

"I don't believe a fuckin' thing that's comin' from your mouth."

I can't help myself, and I know I should probably be thinking a little more clearly about what I'm doing, but I'm so furious. "It's not my fuckin' problem if you do or not. It's the God's honest truth. Whether you believe me or not isn't on me. You should know me better than this, than whatever you think it is I'm capable of. This club is my fuckin' life, and why am I the only one that everyone's accusing of bein' the rat? I'm not the only one fuckin' a woman."

"You're not just fuckin' any broad on the street, son. You're in Mabel Castro's bed, and you know how bad that looks," Ice chimes in, taking a step away from me with the rebar in his hands.

"Armor, come on. You know me better than anyone. You know I would never turn my back on the club." Armor stares at me as I speak, and I watch him swallow hard. He doesn't like doing this, but he's here because Breaker deemed it to be so.

Armor walks away, and the clicking of his combat boots against the floor slowly fades away in the distance. There's a creak of the door opening, and then it slams shut.

"I'd never betray this club or the people in it. Not like you have, strippin' us all of our patches, makin' us feel like you can't trust any of us. I didn't turn my back on this club, Breaker. You did. You turned your back on all of us," I roar, thrashing in my seat because the reality is I'll be dead by the end of the day.

I don't see myself getting out of this, and if I somehow manage to get out . . . I won't ever forgive Breaker for what he's done and what he's going to do.

CHAPTER FOURTEEN

MABEL

I wake up for the third time in the middle of the night to check my phone. Ops still hasn't called or texted me back. I know I wanted to try and give him some space, but now I'm really starting to get worried.

After the girls left from my small breakdown, I took a nice long bath and had myself some ice cream. When Ops didn't call by the time I went to bed, I sent him another text message. I expected him to hit me back after that, but he hasn't. It's not like him to go so long without checking in. He and I have been basically inseparable since we got together, so to have him all of a sudden just up and leave without reaching out to me for the day is jarring, to say the least.

I call his phone now, and it just rings until it gets to voicemail. I don't leave one. Instead, I sit up in bed and cross my arms over my chest. If he's playing some type of game with me, I'm going to be so fucking pissed off. I don't have any time to deal with anyone else trying to fuck with my emotions right now. I need to stay focused on making sure that I do what I can to find out where Ops is.

There's no way that I'm going to be able to go back to sleep now, so I get out of bed and walk over to my small desk, and power up my laptop. I don't know much about where he says he works, but I did see a patch on his leather. Maybe I can find some information about that, I'd be able to find him that way. I didn't know the name of the club, and now that I've been looking through all the different patches, something makes me think that I should have gotten that fact from him. There are a lot of other clubs and not all of them are good people, according to the various police reports that I managed to dig up.

Finally, after searching for about an hour, I found one that looked like the one I'd seen on Ops leather. Once I get the name of the motorcycle club that he's in, I do a reverse search to see if I can find a location or phone number. I try to call the number that I see, but no one picks up.

I sit and wait for a few to see if he's going to text me back, but after another ten minutes with no communication from him, I'm in the shower and getting dressed. It's not like me to go chasing after anyone, but I just need to make sure he's okay. If he is okay, I'm going to punch him in the face for making me worry.

I don't get the location of the actual clubhouse, but I do see that they own a bar that's not far from my house, but the minute I get there, I'm a little scared. I've never been to a place like this, and I've come all by my lonesome. That might not have been the best idea.

Suddenly the night I was kidnapped and beaten as a message to my father replays in my mind. What if these guys are like that? What if they're not all like Ops. He could not be there at all, and then I could be walking right into a lion's den.

My breathing starts to come faster, and I realize I'm about to have a fucking panic attack just thinking about all the what if's.

"Stop it. You're going to be fine," I say to myself, doing my best to muster up some courage. I get out of the car and make my way to what I'm assuming is the front door. It's still pretty late in the middle of the night, so there's every chance that it could be completely deserted this time of night. Even so, I see a few lights on, so I'm going to go out on a limb and say they're still open for business.

I try to open the door straight out, but it doesn't budge. I knock, and a man with one of the leathers that I saw Ops wearing opens the door for me. It's obvious that he's not expecting someone to be coming in this late at night, but he lets me in any way. I take a step inside and scan the inside of the bar. There are a few people inside, but nothing looks out of the ordinary. There are people with the same vest on in here as well, so that makes me think they'd know something about Ops.

I hope they do, at least.

I lift my chin, stick my hands in my pockets and walk over to the bar, where there is a young Filipino man standing behind it. He wipes down the bar, and when I sit down in front of him, the most he does is squint his eyes at me. I'm not sure what kind of business he has, but most people that own a business want to sell their merchandise. This bartender didn't even ask me if I wanted anything to drink.

"You closed for the night or something?" I ask, finally finding my voice.

"No, sweet thing, but I don't think you came all the way over here in the middle of the night for something to drink. You want something, so why not just get on with it." The bartender crosses his arms over his chest.

I want to get snippy with him, but he's right. I am here for something. "Fine, I wanted to know if Ops was here."

Instantly the nonchalant smirk that he's wearing on his face drops off, and he squints his eyes at me. "Why the hell are you in here looking for him? How do you know him?"

Crap, Ops and I have never really had the labels talk. What am I supposed to tell this man? Maybe he didn't want any of his friends to know that he was with me. It's too late to worry about that now, "We're dating. He's been staying with me, but I haven't heard from him all night. I'm worried," I admit, even though it makes me sound weak as hell.

"Hmm." That's all he says, but then he cocks his brow and looks over to the blond man that is sitting all the way at the other end of the bar. I assume that he wants me to go talk to him, but it would have been much easier if he had just opened his mouth to say that. Much politer too.

Jumping down from the stool, I walk over to the man with blond hair who has yet to look in my direction.

"Chains," the man behind the bar calls him, "This is Ops' girl. She's looking for him."

Chains stops what he's doing and turns his gaze on me. I have to stop myself from moving away. He seems a little scary. More so than the rest of the people in here. There's nothing wrong with him per se, just something about his demeanor that makes me think he's a little bit on the savage side.

"Come on," Chains says, and I follow him to the back, all the while my heart beating a million miles a minute in my chest.

"Where are you taking me?" I ask when the area I'm walking through starts to get darker.

"You need to talk to Breaker."

Who the hell is Breaker, and what the hell is up with these names? Chains, Ops, Breaker. All of them make me want to run and hide.

We knock on the door of an office, and when I walk in, there is yet another man who is not Ops sitting behind a desk. A tall brunette man stands and looks at me. He's not as big as the one that brought me back here. Instead, he's built more like a swimmer. Still, he's intimidating.

"You Breaker?" I ask, and he nods his head.

"I am. I'm also the president of this club, and I have a few questions for you." He glares at me, and suddenly, I'm not feeling very safe at all.

"Questions? Why do you need to ask me anything? All I want to know is if anyone has seen him." I take a step back, trying to get closer to the door in case I have to run, but the bigger man, Chains, is still standing behind me.

"Yeah, I heard that part already. What I want to know is what Ops told you." Breaker leans forward against the desk, and I cringe away.

"What are you talking about? Tell me about what?"

Breaker slams his hand down on the table, "Don't play with me, girl! Tell me what he's told you about us, or things are going to end badly for you."

I should have known better than to just come in here with no type of protection, especially if I didn't know that Ops was here. "Look, Breaker, I don't know what you're talking about. Ops never tells me anything. I didn't even know you were a damn motorcycle club until this evening. I had to do a fucking reverse image search on your patch to even find this bar. Whatever you're thinking he's telling me, you're wrong," I snap back at him.

Neither one of them has told me where Ops is, and if they're going through all this drama to keep me from seeing him, then I don't think he's got the best friends in the world. Breaker stares at me over his desk for a little while longer, trying to intimidate me, but I've been through worse.

"You going to tell me where he is or not?" I ask, making sure to keep my chin raised high.

He walks around his desk and stands right in front of me, "Yeah, we'll go see him, but I promise you, every-thing you said better fucking pan out." He grabs me by the arm and pulls me toward the door.

I don't know where he's taking me, but I'm hoping Ops is nearby. I can't deal with another group of people trying to beat me down. This time, I don't think there's going to be anyone to come find me.

CHAPTER FIFTEEN

OPS

I don't even know long I've been gone. It might be hours, could be days with how disoriented I've been feeling. Who knows, it might've only been a few hours. After taking this many hits to the face, nothing is making sense anymore. I'm in a room with no windows, and the only semblance of light I have is from the hallway. It never goes off, and I see it at all hours of the day.

Heavy footsteps grow closer, and I inhale deeply. I wonder who it is, but I've only been seeing Ice and Breaker since I've been here. I have to be in a storage closet in the basement of *The Clubhouse*.

We have a working bar at the front of the club. Our actual clubhouse for the Satan's Raiders MC is in the same building as the bar, and the only people who work at the bar are prospects, patch bunnies, or clubwhores. We don't have any clubwhores right now, but I remember a few months back, Breaker was looking to get a couple. He doesn't like that the prospects are always working at the bar and not doing enough shit for the club.

The bar isn't a massive space. There's enough for maybe sixty or seventy people to sit down, and our kitchen isn't overly large. It gets the job done, and that's what matters. Everyone has rooms above the bar, and behind the bar is where Breaker's office is. Downstairs is where we have our main area, storage closets, and more. I'm going to bet that's where Breaker has me, in one of the closets. Normally I'd be able to tell a lot sooner, but none of the brothers have been here as much since Breaker stripped us all of our patches.

Footsteps grow closer, and the door to the room I'm in is suddenly thrown open. The light turns on, and I blink a few times, adjusting to the sudden brightness. After my eyes settle down, I'm shocked to see who Breaker has with him, or rather, whose arm he's got a death grip on.

She gasps the second she sees me.

"Has he hurt you?" I immediately question her, ready to kill the man who I formerly thought of as a friend.

Breaker shoves her into the room, releasing her arm in the process. "No, he'd never dare to attempt such a thing," Mabel tells me, and I smile. She's my woman and a hell of one at that. She's well-rounded, intelligent, and sassy as fuck. "But he did this to you, didn't he?"

I don't confirm what she's asked, but Mabel knows he did this to me. There's no other option.

"What happened to you, Ops?" Mabel questions, taking a few steps closer to me until her fingertips are tracing against my cheek. She's touching the side where the rebar hit, the same side where I think my cheekbone is broken.

"Nothing I can't handle," I tell her, but my eyes are locked on Breaker. He'd better pray she convinces me to get out of here without making a fuss because all I want to do is break his fucking head in.

Mabel turns and glares right at Breaker. "You did this, didn't you?"

Breaker doesn't bother responding to her, which I know is only going to piss her off even more.

"Why in the hell would you do something like this? Look at him!" Mabel shrieks, anger evident in her tone.

"Rats don't belong in my club, Ms. Castro." Breaker speaks so matter-of-factly like there isn't a doubt in his mind. He really thinks I betrayed the club, and it only makes me angrier. It feels like my eyes are about to bulge out of my head and sweat goes down the back of my neck.

Mabel raises her brows at Breaker's statement. "What rats?" she doesn't know anything about the situation here, and I doubt Breaker will fill her in.

"It's none of your concern, Ms. Castro." Breaker's making it a point to speak to her in a monotone manner, and I'm taking notice of it. I'm sure Mabel is as well, and I'm sure it's pissing her off the more he does it.

"I don't know what in the fuck you think it is that he's told me, but Ops doesn't tell me anything about the club. All I knew was that he was in a brotherhood here. Sure, I saw the vest or cut, but I didn't go digging for information. It's obvious to me that you think I'm somehow part of why he's in that chair. I'm not an idiot. I'll take a fucking polygraph if it makes a differ-ence because I don't have a damn thing to hide."

Breaker looks at Mabel and furrows his brows like he's considering it.

"I wouldn't ever betray the club, and you know it. All of this was senseless, and you're wasting your time while the real rat is still out there. Not to mention, I don't know if I'll ever forgive you for this. There are things we could move past, but I'm not sure this is one of them. Now, I can only imagine the weight that's on your shoulders right now, but I wouldn't do things this way. If you keep doing this, Breaker, you're going to lose your best people. The whole club will walk away if they feel like they can't be trusted, and after this . . . I wouldn't be surprised if they're all gone by the end of the fuckin' week."

"If you think because we've been friends for years that it'll make me treat you differently than anyone else, you're wrong. You're talkin' out your ass 'cause you got caught. That's what's happenin' right now." Breaker again sounds so sure of himself when he has no clue what's going on.

"You're supposed to be friends with him, and this is how you treat Ops? Are you crazy?" Mabel screams, and I notice the tears threatening to spill from her eyes. She barely cries, but I know this isn't easy for her. It's evident to me here and now that she feels as deeply for me as I feel for her.

"My club comes above all else, but I don't owe you an explanation. You're not part of my club."

"She might not be part of the club, but she's my ol' lady, and you'll treat her with the same damn respect as you treat any other," I snarl at Breaker, and he lifts his chin understanding the magnitude of what I've said. Though, Mabel doesn't have a clue what it means.

"I didn't betray the club. I would never betray the club because, if nothing else, the club is all that I have. Why would I go against the very place that keeps me sane? Ask yourself that question. What could I have to gain by hurting the only family I've ever had?" The Satan's Raiders MC is my only family, the only family I've had in years after I turned my back on my blood. They weren't anything special. They were far from it. They were toxic people who only wanted me for money, so I walked away. I cut them off, and it was the best decision I ever made.

The door opens again, and Chains comes into the room. He looks at Mabel, then me, then to Breaker. "Prez, we gotta talk."

"It can wait," Breaker tells Chains.

"No, it can't." Chains is adamant and leaves the room immediately, then Breaker follows him.

Mabel comes up to me and pulls something from her bra, and it's a utility knife. She flips it open and brings the knife against the zip ties that've been on my wrists since the warehouse. Mabel pulls the blade against the zip tie until it breaks, and suddenly the pressure around my wrists isn't so strained.

"God, are you okay? And don't you dare lie to me," Mabel says, worry filling her eyes. She looks all over me like she's counting every cut, abrasion, and bruise.

"I'm fine, baby. It's gonna take a lot more than this to take me out, trust me."

Mabel laughs softly, and I'm grateful I was able to lighten the mood a little bit.

I rise and put my arm around Mabel, but we take one step and realize how bad off I am. I'm limping heavily, putting most of my weight on my right leg. My left is messed up from when Ice slammed the rebar down on my left leg. I didn't think the damage was that bad, but I was wrong.

The door to the storage closet opens, and Breaker pauses in the doorway. He breathes in heavily and releases it before he speaks. "I was coming to do that."

I want to call bullshit, but he has his knife out. "What, you get a sudden change of heart?"

"Something like that, sure," Breaker mutters, then looks at the ground. He was so sure I was the person behind this, but I'll guarantee that something else happened while I was here, which means I'm not the one behind this.

"You could've handled this so much better, brother. Instead, you've ruined everything," I comment, and Mabel walks by my side, helping me up the stairs. Once I'm on the main floor, we head toward the back, planning on exiting through the alley. Though, a few of the brothers see me and shake their heads.

"This has gotta be a fuckin' joke," Killer says, and I lock eyes with him. I wish it was a joke. I wish I was never brought into this damn situation, but I was.

"Doesn't look like it," Sarge adds, also disappointed by Breaker's actions.

"I'm out. I'm done with this shit. If this is what's gonna happen to us, I don't wanna be here anymore," Brick speaks up, shaking his head as he heads out the back door. Killer and Sarge follow in his footsteps, and Chains comes up to me.

He places a hand on my shoulder. "You know I had no part in this, but I'm sorry it happened. He thought he was right, but we know he was wrong now."

"Yeah, a little too late for him to realize he was wrong. Don't you think?" Mabel chimes in, and Chains smirks.

"Yeah, I'd say so," he tells her.

"How's your mom doin'? I meant to ask the other day when I got back from the warehouse, but I've been a bit preoccupied."

Chains' smirk falls immediately. "She passed away peacefully in her sleep this morning."

"I am so sorry for your loss," Mabel tells him immediately.

"Thank you. It was better this way. She's been suffering for a long time," Chains tells her, and Mabel becomes tight-lipped.

"I'm still so sorry to hear, but at least she's in a better place now." It's bullshit, but I won't make it seem like I think it is.

"You're right. She's with my grandmother now, and I'm sure she's happy to be reunited with her again," Chains adds. "Anyway, go relax. I'll text you later and let you know what's happening if you're still part of the club . . ." he pauses, awaiting some sort of answer.

"I am . . . for now, but I don't know if I will be for long," I admit, and every bit of what I've said is the truth.

Mabel walks with me out the door and thank God we're not too far away from her apartment. I'm going to wave down a taxi when we get to the main street because all I want to be is in her bed, holding her flush against my body. That's the only thing that will fix what I've been through, and no one will ever be able to convince me of anything different.

CHAPTER SIXTEEN

MABEL

When I wake up the next morning and feel Ops beside me, all I want is to go back to sleep and snuggle closer to him. After all the shit that I saw last night with his club, I'm just glad I got him back to me in one piece. That president of his is completely out of his mind for thinking Ops could go against him. I would think for someone who is supposed to know him so well, he'd realize being a fucking traitor just isn't in Ops' genetic makeup.

Being dictated to isn't in my makeup, either. I let out a groan as I slip from under his arm and head to the bathroom. I'm going to have to get this over with sooner or later. I've been putting off talking to my father since that day he came over to my house, but I can't keep doing that.

I give Ops a kiss goodbye after I've gotten dressed, and I tell him that I'm going to go see my father. Of course, he wanted to come with me, but I knew that if he showed up there with me, it'd only be that much more difficult when it came time to actually talk to him.

"I got this. Keep the bed warm for me," I tell him before I gather the last remaining bits of patience that I have and go over to Hollywood Hills. Back to the one place that I thought I'd never set foot in again. My father's house.

As I walk into his house, I'm a little amazed at how unimpressed I am with it. When I was younger, I thought it was pretty decent—nice size, great amenities, and more than enough space for me to go wherever I wanted in the house and still feel like I had privacy. Now when I walk in, all I see is a big area of nothingness. I wonder how my father hasn't gotten unbearably lonely after all these years.

I didn't bother to give my father a heads-up when I started my trek over to see him, so when I appeared at the door of his study, his eyes went wide.

"Amabel?" He stands at his desk and glares at me. "I didn't know you were coming to visit today. Is there something I can do for you?" he asks, clearly annoyed that I'm here without letting him know first.

"Dad, I came here to talk to you." I sit down in the chair right in front of his desk. I'm going to try and make this as painless as possible. There was a time in my life when he was an okay father to me. I hate that we've fallen out this far.

He takes a seat back in his chair and waits for me to say what it is I have to say.

"I've debated coming over to talk to you about this for the past few weeks now, even before all that kidnapping mess happened. You can't keep trying to force this marriage on me because you think it fulfills some sort of familial obligation. Just because that's what they did in the old country doesn't mean that's the norm here."

He chuckles lightly and shakes his head, and leans forward in his chair, "Mabel, you honestly think I'm asking your opinion on the matter? I'm only allowing you the time to get your head wrapped around the idea. This is how it's done in our family. All cartel daughters go and marry who the boss chooses? I've already made a choice. It's happening."

Slowly, the dots begin to connect in my head. He chose. Does that mean he's the boss of the entire fucking cartel? Is that why I never really knew what he did? "Dad . . . are you saying you run the entire cartel?"

He smiles, "You should be proud. Excited even. You just found out you're a princess."

I can see in his eyes that he means every word he's saying. He thinks this marriage is a fucking done deal. He really believes no matter what I say or do, I'm just going to give up my freedom because of who I'm related to?

"Dad, this is ridiculous. I'm never going to be that type of woman. The woman who will just bow down because some man says so. You should know you've raised me. Did you think all of a sudden, when I hit a certain age, things would change? Because it doesn't change a thing besides the fact that I want more freedoms than before. People don't do this kind of thing anymore. I mean, really, look what year it is!"

He jumps up from his chair and slams his hand down on the desk, "I don't give a fuck what year it is or what you're used to. I am your father, and you are my property until I deem it the appropriate time to hand you off to another. Now I've been more than lenient with you, Mabel, letting you run around and do shit that most other fathers would see as disrespectful. You're not just some cartel member's daughter. You're the bosses' daughter. I run all of it. If I can't keep you in line, what's to stop those that work for me from thinking I can't keep them in line either? No, enough is enough. You've had more freedom than most, and if you don't wise the hell up and realize that I'm giving you the best you're going to get in this situation, then I might just move this wedding closer than you'd like."

I feel the tears gathering behind my eyelids, and I force myself not to cry. How can he do something like this to me? I'm his kid. "I'm your child, your daughter, not a fucking trafficking victim. You can't just do this to me!" I yell at him, my voice becoming a high-pitched screech.

I watch my father in shock as he pulls his hand back and smacks me across the face.

"You're in hysterics, Amabel. Maybe you should come back when you see reason," he tells me, and I place a hand on my warmed cheek before I turn and storm out of his office.

"Don't come back until you do!" he says loud enough for me to hear as I slam the door closed behind me. I run out of his house and jump right back into my car, trying to wrap my head around the fact that I not only just found out that my father is the head of the cartel, but this arranged marriage he's trying to push isn't just some cultural or religious thing, it's mandatory.

I beat my hands against the steering wheel in frustration. I bring my hand up to my face to feel the area I'm sure is turning red on my cheek. That one smack is enough for me to know that I've lost my father now as well as my mother. I'm parentless.

I bang my head against my steering wheel and let myself cry at the thought.

I don't want to go back to Ops like this. He'll want to come over here and take things up with my dad. I can't bear to lose him too.

I try to call Celia, but she doesn't answer. I groan but quickly move on to Puma. Seems like Celia is always missing nowadays.

Puma answers the phone on the first ring, and when she hears my voice, she tells me to come over right away.

The entire drive there, my eyes are blurry from all the crying. The second I make it to her apartment, she rips open the door and pulls me into her arms. For the second time in as many weeks, she's been here to hold me while I cried.

I update her on all that happened at my father's house about how he's not just a part of the Guatemalan cartel, that he's the boss. I told her how he basically told me that it didn't matter what I wanted, that I was going to marry who he told me to marry, and she had the nerve to smirk.

"What's so funny?" I ask.

"Mabel, yeah, your father's a super dick, but you don't need to worry. Nothing's going to happen that you don't want to happen. I mean, this is my brother he's talking about, remember."

I sit up straight. That's true. My father has made plans for me to marry Silas, but her brother already knows that's not what I want. "I'm lucky it's your brother."

Puma nods her head and drapes a hand over my shoulder, "Silas won't come near you until you say. If you even say so in the first place. You have nothing to worry about."

Finally, I breathe a sigh of relief. This is truly a draining experience. I look at my watch and notice how late it's getting. I've got a man at home waiting for me. I don't need to think about this right now. All I need to be thinking about is Ops.

CHAPTER SEVENTEEN

OPS

The elevator doors open, and out comes Mabel, looking worse for wear. Not in a physical sense, though she looks like she's about to pull out that utility knife she keeps tucked away in her bra and slit some-one's throat.

At first, I don't say anything because I'm not sure if she needs me right now. I'm unsure if she wants to be alone with her feelings or if she wants to vent. She kicks off her shoes and heads for the kitchen, wasting no time as she opens her freezer and pulls out her favorite bottle of rum. Whatever happened, she's furi-ous. She has her lips pinched together in a tight line, and her posture's as rigid as ever.

"Do you wanna talk about it, or are you gonna just drink away your problems?" I realize how bad it sounds as soon as it passes my lips, and Mabel glares at me with all of her might.

She opens her mouth and then smacks her lips shut, clenching her jaw in the process. Mabel proceeds to pour herself a drink and taps her fingertips against the counter. When she's finished, she places the bottle on the counter and downs the shot. "The last thing I need right now is your attitude, so either fix it or don't say a damn thing to me." She's speaking quickly like emotion is flooding through her body. I don't know if she's angry or if she's about to cry.

"I'm sorry, baby. I didn't mean for that to come out the way it did, I promise. I'm just tryin' to help you sort out whatever's goin' on. I went about it the wrong way, sounded like a total ass and everything." I could've thought about what I was going to say a little bit better, but I didn't, and I stuck my foot in my damn mouth.

Mabel inhales deeply through her nose and then nods. "Yeah, you sounded like a total jackass."

"I know I did," I pause for a few moments and wait for Mabel to say something else, but she doesn't. "Do you want to talk about it?"

Mabel pours herself another shot and takes it back before she says a word. "My father is the most idiotic man to ever walk the Earth. Of that, I'm certain."

Fuck, so this has to do with her father. Mabel isn't the type of woman to have daddy issues, not by any means, but she is strong-willed and obviously furious about something.

"There's something else goin' on here, sweetheart. You can speak in riddles, or you could tell me what's bothering you so much."

Mabel pours herself another drink and takes a shot, then presses her back against the counter, plants her hands on it, and looks right at me. "My father arranged a marriage for me like I'm some woman stuck in the 1800s. He didn't ask my opinion or even speak to me about the matter. He just did it, and he acts like it won't matter like I'm going to do whatever he says. Granted, the man he arranged this marriage with is my best friend's brother, but I'm not doing it. It's why there's been a wedge between my father and me for years because he doesn't understand the severity of what he's trying to do. It's ridiculous!" Mabel has a white-knuckled grip on the counter and finally releases it.

I'm still processing everything she's told me. "Let me get this straight . . . your father arranged a marriage for you?"

Mabel blinks at me a few times like she doesn't understand why I'm asking her to reiterate. "Yes, he did."

Her father arranged a marriage for her, and she thinks she has a choice in the matter? This isn't how cartel families work. If your father arranges a marriage for you, you get married. The women don't have a choice. "Fuckin' hell . . ." I mutter, running my palm over my face in complete disbelief. I've been shacking up with a woman who's already promised to someone else.

Cartel leaders are the type of men who will literally have their daughters tied down and raped so their marriages are consummated. Chances that she's going to get out of this are slim to none. It won't happen. There's no way. "I'm not marrying him, Ops."

I meet my eyes with Mabel's and cock a brow. "Do you seriously think you're gettin' out of it?"

Mabel nods almost immediately. "I do because I'm not a pawn in my father's game. I never have been, and I never will be. Plus, I've been seeing this guy who I really like. A man who I'd like to see by my side for a long time to come if he wants me too."

I think she's crazy as fuck for standing up against her father but being with Mabel is the only thing I want. I want her in my life for the rest of my days. I've already called her my ol' lady, and it's because she is. She's the

type of ride-or-die chick that will do whatever's necessary for her man, and I already know she'll be a great
mother. Fuck, why am I even thinking about her being
a mother right now? Probably because it's so natural
for me to imagine it.

"I called you my ol' lady earlier, sweetheart. I'm not
lettin' you go." I break the distance between us until
I'm standing directly in front of her body.

"What does that mean? Ol' lady?" Mabel furrows her
brows a bit, and I cackle.

"It means you're with me until the end, and I'm with
you for just as long. It means I protect you with my life,
and you'll be here to patch up my wounds when I have
'em. It means you're my entire world and that I'm not
just gonna walk out on you. It means you're my everything, Mabel Castro."

Mabel blinks a couple of times, and a smile tugs at the
corner of her lips. "Well, that's a lot to live up to,
isn't it?"

"You don't have to live up to anythin', baby. You're
already there," I murmur as I grow closer to her plump
lips. I graze mine against hers until she's matching my
pace, but I make the next move. I crash my lips against
her own, kissing her in a way that I haven't ever kissed
her before. This kiss between us feels different than the

rest. It feels like it means more because we've solidified everything. I meant every word I said to her: she is my world. I don't know what I'd be without her in my life because I don't know how I ever got by without her before.

My phone rings in my back pocket, which causes me to break our kiss. Chains' name pops up on the screen, so I bring it to my ear. "I figured you'd be out of town by now."

"Sadly, no. My extended family can't be here for her services yet. I planned it for two weeks away, which gives me some time to handle things here, hopefully."

"If we can get this shit handled with the club in two weeks, it'll be a damn miracle," I tell Chains, and I'm being serious. It's been going on for God knows how long.

"Yeah, so I have an idea. The club hasn't been much of a club for a bit now. This rat shit is really ruining every-thing. I want everyone in the club in an hour, including you. Bring your ol' lady if you want. I'm gonna have Hammer there too." Hammer is the regent from the Reapers Rejects MC's Montana charter. He's been here for a little bit now, and Inc's been up in Montana as our regent for a while.

"Why are we gonna have Hammer in on this? He's not part of the Satan's Raiders." I don't understand Chains' thought process, but it's interesting to me that Chains is the one calling the shots.

"I think we need some outside input, don't you? We need someone else's eyes on everyone. Someone who we trust."

He isn't wrong. Hammer doesn't know shit besides things within the Satan's Raiders have been tense as of late. "You bet. I'll be there in thirty minutes," I tell Chains and hang up the phone.

"What's going on?" Mabel asks, drawing her brows together.

"We're going to the club in a bit. You're invited, considerin' you're my ol' lady." I smirk as I say it and collide my lips with hers.

Mabel breaks the kiss. "You said we'd be there in thirty minutes . . . but we could be there sooner than that."

"Yeah, I wanna show my woman just how much I care about her," I whisper against her lips, staring into those beautiful eyes of hers.

"But your leg. You should probably give it a couple of days."

"I know my dick is big, but it isn't a leg, baby."

Mabel smacks me on the shoulder. "I'm not talking about that! You're *actual* leg."

"It'll be just fine, baby. Come on, we're wasting time." I grab her hand and drag her ass toward the bed. We'll have to be quick, but I'm sure we can both get what we need before we head over to the club.

CHAPTER EIGHTEEN

This is the second time that I've been in the clubhouse, and honestly, this time, it's been a much better experience. Even the big man, Chains, isn't as terrifying as he was the first time I saw him.

We've only been here about ten minutes when the door to the clubhouse opens, and even though no one immediately reaches for weapons, I see them all tense a slight bit. All of them are ready to jump into action.

Breaker's the first one in, and everyone relaxes. I look away back to Ops, and I'm surprised to hear a familiar girl's voice coming from behind Breaker. When I look again, I see there's a woman behind him.

She comes in fully, and I'm so surprised that I stand up and stare at her.

"Celia?" I squeak out.

Celia turns in my direction, and she looks absolutely terrified. I swear if she wasn't clenched up so tight, she would've just shit her pants.

"That's not her name. This is Cee, my girlfriend," Breaker says.

"Her name is Celia," I repeat it again, and everyone goes quiet.

The tension in the room is thick, and suddenly, I think I just stumbled on something that I shouldn't have.

Ops comes up behind me. "What's your full name?" he asks her.

She clears her throat and, after a second, she speaks, "Celia."

Breaker goes silent and stares at her. He cocks one of his eyebrows up, and his jaw is clenched tight. That dangerous man that I met the other day is back, and I'm starting to think maybe Celia isn't free to say what's going on.

I take another step closer to her, completely worried that perhaps she's in some sort of trouble now, and she needs me to get her out.

I mean, the first time I met Breaker, he wasn't the nicest person, so maybe he's keeping her here against her will? "What are you doing here?" I ask her. "It's been a long time. Have you been here the whole time?" I think back on the last couple of times I asked her to come over or to go out and how she said she couldn't make it or she had to leave early.

Her eyes widen, and I see her walking toward me. I meet her halfway and pull her into a hug. She's my best friend, we've always hugged before. Just as I'm about to let go, she places her lips to my ear and whispers.

"Shut the hell up before you get me killed."

I let her go, and suddenly, I feel sick to my stomach. Something *is* wrong. I snap my mouth shut and walk back over to where Ops is. I see him out the corner of my eye, trying to catch my gaze, but I don't look back up.

"Come on, babe, let's get out of here." Celia tries to get Breaker to leave, and Ops shakes me a little, trying to figure out why I'm so upset.

Breaker is glaring at me again. This time instead of him saying anything to me, he turns to look at Celia. "Sure, we can go, but first, I want to know how you two know each other." I look at Celia to see what she says. If she's going to lie or not. When she doesn't say anything right away, I know this is about to be a fucking shitshow.

Breaker turns to stare at me. "You answer. How do you two know each other?" When I look up into my friend's face, I can see that she's pissed. I don't know why. She's acting like I'm the one who got her into whatever mess she's in. There should be no reason why she should have to hide who she is from Breaker.

"We've known each other since we were little girls. Our fathers are friends."

Breaker's eyes go from me to Celia and back again.

"Guatemalan?" Breaker asks, and I nod yes. He points to Celia, and I nod yes again.

He backs up from her, and I see the hurt rush across his features before his face turns into a mask of pure fucking rage, "You're the fuckin' rat."

Oh no.

Celia immediately gets down on her knees and starts to beg. He's right. It is her.

"Breaker, babe, please, you don't understand. Don't kill me. I didn't have a choice. I was so torn between being an MC queen by your side and pleasing my father."

"What? You were conflicted?" Breaker's voice is like acid as it slides from between his lips. I watch in disgust as he spits directly in my friend's face. "A real ol' lady would never have that fuckin' problem. You would stand by your man through thick and thin, no matter what fuckin' outside influences there are. Ain't this about a fucking bitch?" Breaker tosses his hands up and turns away from her, "Agony, Fury, come get this piece of shit and get her out of my sight until I figure out what the fuck to do with her."

Oh, this is bad. I look over at Ops to let him know that this is going to get worse if Celia doesn't go home. Her father will come for her, and there will be a bloodbath.

The two men pick Celia up, and instantly my friend starts to scream and curse. Her previous stance of being sorry and trying to gain sympathy is already done.

"You won't get away with this. You don't know what you're dealing with. I'm important!"

Breaker surges toward her. "You're not as fuckin' important as you think. You're not irreplaceable."

"Bullshit, I'm not. I'm the leader of the 17's daughter," she yells out, and I suck in a deep breath.

I step forward and stare at her. "Your father's position can't protect you forever, Celia. You have no idea what he's done and how your decision to tell your father things impacted others."

Celia swings her head in my direction, her eyes squinted into slits, "You stupid, ignorant bitch. You think you're so high and mighty because your father's a dealer? No, you're nobody. You shouldn't be the one talking to me like this. Not when you don't even support your father's lifestyle. You act like you don't know what he does, but we all know what you've been doing, Amabel. You're lying to yourself because you can't face the truth. You can't face that your entire family made their money selling drugs. I'm a daughter who appreciates their father. I was the first one to help him clear the streets of the trash. The one to bring him the asshole drug dealers who went against him." There's a deep gasp around the room, and I watch Breaker take out his gun.

"You! You're the fucking one who told him? Those dealers your father is responsible for killing were dads. They have kids. Your father destroyed lives, and then you fucking come in here and lay in my fuckin' bed! You don't fuckin' deserve to live! You don't get to fucking breathe anymore." His words are soft at the end, and even though I can see the struggle in his expression, Breaker pulls the trigger, shooting a bullet straight through my best friend's head.

I watch in a daze as her body goes limp and then hits the floor with a sick *thud*. I knew her for most of my life, and I never once knew that she had no morals or that she could be the fucking reason Ops club was going through so much. Even in her death, Celia will be the cause of more problems because once her father finds out that it was the Satan's Raiders that killed her, nothing is going to stop him from coming after all of them. Ops included.

CHAPTER NINETEEN

OPS

The door opens, and Breaker walks in with his gaze on the ground. He's disappointed in himself, and it's obvious as hell. Because of the whole situation with Celia, we shut *The Clubhouse* down. We all needed to be together as a club, reconnect, and all that shit.

Breaker runs a hand over his head and brings it down over the back of his neck. He finally looks at the group of us and clears his throat. "I don't even know what to say, brothers. I fucked up, and I fucked up pretty bad."

Ice is sitting next to Killer at the bar and turns his seat around to face his son. "You did what you thought was best."

Breaker shakes his head. "Don't try to make me feel like what I did was right. It wasn't. I should've trusted my club before anyone else. I should've realized I was letting things slip when I was with *her*."

Shit, he can't even say Celia's name. This is bad, really bad. If Mabel had done the same to me, I don't know if I'd be able to say her name either.

"You're right," Chains speaks up, pushing himself off the wall he's been leaning against. "You did fuck up, and royally at that. The thing is, we might all say we'd act in a different way, but none of us actually know it. We could've done the same thing as you, Breaker. Breathe, man. It was a difficult situation to deal with in the first place."

Now that we all know who's responsible for the dealer's being killed, our location being scavenged, and money being stolen . . . we're trying to give Breaker a break. I don't know if he deserves it, given the way he was treating us, but it just goes to show that the club comes before all else.

"Don't make excuses for me. I should've seen this coming from a mile away. I didn't know her, and I was being so careless," Breaker tells everyone, and Mabel clears her throat.

"She targeted you. She made you feel like you could trust her with anything and everything, and as much as I hate what you did to him, you were being manipulated by one of the best in the game. Her father's trained her how to do this since she was a small child." Something in Mabel's voice makes me think she's analyzing every aspect of her friendship, or former friendship, with Cee.

"I *should* have seen this coming." Breaker doesn't want to believe any of us.

"If it were me, I wouldn't have thought it could be my girl," I speak up, knowing she's the last person I'd want to believe did this. "I would've looked for any other available option, just like you did." The more I think about this, the more I realize I would've probably done exactly what Breaker did. I wanted to think I wouldn't at first . . . but I realized I'm wrong.

"I know you're all just sayin' this shit to make me feel better. I never thought my girl would be behind this shit. It's a sick fuckin' joke." Breaker shakes his head, still in shock from everything we've all discovered.

"Chill, brother. It's all over and done with now. This is all part of the past," Armor speaks up, causing everyone to nod in agreement with his statement.

"It's not in the past. I need to make things right now. Firstly, all of you are hereby reinstated back into your positions. I'm so sorry for ever stripping you of your patches. I know now just how wrong I was in doing so." Breaker makes sure to keep eye contact with every person in the room, even Hammer, who isn't even part of our club.

"Life is about learning, and this was a great lesson for everyone involved," Hammer speaks up, and all of us nod. He's right. This was a huge lesson.

"You're right. Fury, Agony," Breaker pauses and turns to the two prospects in the club, "I think you two have proven yourself through this entire ordeal. While I'm reinstating everyone else, I'm officially makin' the two of you full patches."

The only people in *The Clubhouse* right now are the members of the club, Mabel, and Hammer.

"If Fury and Agony are now fully patched members, who are we gonna have doin' the grunt work around here?" Sarge questions, bringing up a valid point.

"I'll be on the lookout for new prospects, but I think this shouldn't just be a decision I make. If any of you see men with potential, bring them in, and we'll see if they stick," Breaker tells everyone.

We all look at each other, and things finally feel like they're beginning to get normal again. While all of this shit was going on, Breaker would've never given us the leeway for something like this.

"My brother, he would benefit from this life. He's in rehab right now . . . I went in a few days ago, right before our mother passed. He doesn't need to be back home with the same shit tempting him. He's got no real support system out there. If you're all okay with it, I'd like to bring him out here when he gets released." Chains speaks up.

I didn't even know he had a brother. All I ever heard about was his mother.

"Yeah, man. Of course," Breaker tells him.

Ice slides off his barstool and takes a few steps toward Chains. "If he needs a sponsor, I can be that man. I'll try to keep him on the straight and narrow, 'cause Lord knows it can be difficult with all this temptation everywhere."

"I appreciate that, brother. Thank you," Chains replies.

The group of us begin to dissipate, and shortly enough, *The Clubhouse* is back and open for business. Chains sits next to Mabel and me, and Fury's behind the bar tending to the customers.

"Now that you're not a prospect anymore, who in the hell is gonna clean my bike?" Chains asks Fury, who has a shit-eating grin crossing his face. He loves the fact he's no longer a prospect, and I think he and his brother rightfully earned their place as full patch men.

"Dunno, man," Fury snickers.

"If you need someone to clean your pipes, I can volunteer as tribute," a sassy redhead says from a few barstools down.

If Chains was a normal man, he probably would smile and flirt back . . . but the woman he loved was killed a few years ago. That woman happened to be one of Breaker's sisters. She was his everything, even if he hadn't really admitted it yet. After a trauma like that, you can't expect any man to be the same. I know I wouldn't be if Mabel was in Xia's shoes. I don't even know how he's gotten this far, because I can imagine it's like living through hell.

CHAPTER TWENTY

MABEL

My nerves are all over the place as I walk back into the door of my father's house. The last time I was here, I found out some incredibly life-altering news, not to mention he basically told me that I was nothing more than a fucking chess piece in his game. A pawn for him to move around as he saw fit.

It'll never be me.

This time I made sure to let him know that I'd be coming over. I don't want any more surprises besides the one that I already have up my sleeve. The house-maid comes to me and takes my jacket. Her face is grim, which must mean my father's already not in a good mood.

It's no longer my concern. As long as I get what I need to say out, then after I leave here, it'll be the concern of everyone else. My heels click on the floor as I make my way to his office, and I knock on the door. Waiting patiently for him to give me the permission that I need to come in. My stomach flips over at least thirty fucking times before he tells me that I can enter.

"I'm glad to see you've returned," he says the moment I step foot in the office. Though he doesn't look up from his paperwork.

"Yeah, I made a few important decisions that I feel like you should know about."

He drops his pen and raises his head so he can look at me now. I stare into his eyes and am shocked by how different he is. For most of my life, I thought that he was just a complicated and closed-off man. Come to find out, he's nothing more than a cold-blooded killer.

I shake my head in disappointment and take a step forward. I'm not going to let anything distract me from what I need to do.

"Well, go on. What's this decision that you've made?" My father waves his hand, trying to get me to hurry up.

"You should've never made me choose between you and the man I love," I say clearly, and he smiles at me.

"Love is so . . . subjective. Who knows, in a few months, you could learn to love your new husband." He gets out of his chair and comes to stand in front of his desk, a cocky smirk still on his face.

"At the end of the day, someone's going to be hurting, and I hate that you put me in this situation. I want you to be happy, in some twisted way. You just being my father is enough for me to want you to have a good life, but I can't let it dictate mine," I say, and second by second, that smirk on his face drops.

"What are you saying? Speak plainly," he barks out.

"I'm saying I'm going to marry the man that I love. I chose Ops, and there's nothing you can do about it. I'll run down the aisle with him before I let you give me a way to Silas." I keep my back firm and maintain eye contact at all times. My father lives to find a weakness, and he's not going to find one in me today.

"You're being ridiculous. You already know who I am and what people will do to get to me. Do you think that little video they made beating you up is the worst that can happen to you? I promise you it isn't. You're going to become an even bigger target, and I'm not going to be around to save you. The other cartel families will use you as a way to retaliate against me. You'll be on your own." His face turns a darker red, and his hands ball up into fists.

I'm not sure if he's telling me these things because he just doesn't want me to get hurt or because he doesn't want me to go against his word. Either way, I'm going to live my life the way I see fit.

"I'm not going to need any saving from you. I have the club, and all of them have my back. If push came to shove, all of them would go to war for me. I'm not worried about my safety when it comes to them."

His eyes squint slightly before he breaks out into hysterical laughter, "Wait, wait, you mean to tell me you think you're going to be safe in a biker club? That those degenerates and inbred fools are going to be able to do anything when it comes to people in my world coming for you? I promise you'll be dead within the month if you trust them." He flips his hand at me, trying to dismiss what I'm saying, "Amabel, you're an absolute fool if you think that staying at a biker club is what's best for you, and by God, how is my daughter, Amabel Castro, a damned fool?"

Now it's my time to smile. My father doesn't understand the dynamic. He doesn't know that it's not just a fucking club between the lot of them. He doesn't realize that they're a family. I'm a part of that family now, and no matter what, they *are* going to protect me. As long as I stay loyal to them, they're going to stay loyal to me, which is more than I can say for my father and the people that he works with.

"I wish I could be here to see your face when you realize that you're wrong."

He stops laughing and takes a menacing step in my direction. I don't flinch.

"If you walk out of that door, Amabel, I promise you'll regret it. You will no longer be my daughter, and I'll make sure to let everyone know that fact." He says the last part as if it's a fucking threat. I already realized that I lost my father the moment he struck me. A moment I will never forget because I didn't want to be his ready-made whore for sale.

"Be good, Dad," I say, giving him one last glance before I turn and walk out of his office. I don't look back, not because I'm worried he might be angry but because even after all the shit he's done, I don't want to see his reaction. That's my father, and I just gave him up for life.

The ride back to the clubhouse is long, but it goes by in a blur. When I walk in the door, everyone greets me like I'm family. It's bittersweet.

I just walked away from the only man that I ever considered to truly be my family with a promise from him that the rest of my life would be a regret. I walk to the back to find Ops, who's sitting in one of the side rooms by himself, scrolling through his phone.

"Babe?" His eyes pop up to mine when I walk in. He knows what could've happened today. Any time I go see my father, there's a chance that I come back here and tell him that I'm not going to be able to be with him. Up until now, there was always a chance that I wasn't going to be able to deal with the adversity. At least, that is what I think he believes. It's going to take him a little while to figure out that when I'm loyal to someone, it's absolute.

"I hope you meant what you said the other day about me being your ol' lady."

His brows scrunch inward, "Of course I did. I don't say shit like that for kicks. You're mine now. You're always going to be a part of this family, Mabel."

"Well, that's good because you're the only family I have. I let my father know that no matter what, I was going to stay with you. I told him that I'd run down the aisle with you before I let him give me to someone else. I love you, Ops, and I'll give up everything I have to stay with you."

Ops lets out a rough breath and wraps his arms around my waist. "Fuck babe, you serious?"

"As a fucking heart attack." I lace my arms around his neck. "He said you wouldn't be able to protect me from the rest of the cartel . . ."

"Bullshit, no one touches you. You're going to be safe here with me. "

I kiss his lips softly, "I never had a doubt."

He pulls me up on his lap, and I grind down on his already rock-hard cock.

"Fuck, why can't I ever get enough of you."

I chuckle lightly, "I hope that never changes."

"The way I'm fucking obsessed with you, I highly doubt it." His voice is gritty, and he yanks on my thighs, hitching them higher on his waist, so he can carry me to his room.

Once we get inside, he drops me on the bed and slowly begins to strip out of his clothes. I watch him, leaning on my elbows. He grabs hold of my leg when he finishes getting undressed and pulls off my pants.

His head is between my thighs, worshiping and sucking on my clit before I can even open my mouth.

There was never any other choice. The minute Ops came into my life was the minute I became his.

EPILOGUE

OPS

Two Weeks Later . . .

When the time came for Chains to go back to his rural hometown in Louisiana, I wasn't about to let him go alone. Not when he had a mountain of shit to deal with due to his mother's recent passing and his brother being in rehab. He needed support, and I had no problem standing by him and being there for whatever he needed. That's why I'm here with him now because if push came to shove, he'd do the same for me.

But I didn't come alone to support him. Armor and Mabel came with us. We rode from Los Angeles a couple of days ago, and the ride was smooth. We stopped for a night and stayed with the Reapers Rejects MC at their Las Vegas charter and then made the rest of the trip the following day. It was a long ride but well worth it.

Chains had most of his mother's arrangements made, but not all of them had been finalized, so we went with him to the funeral home, burial ground, and anything else he needed. Earlier today, he went to go visit his brother in rehab, and his mother's funeral is tomorrow. He said his brother's being let out for the day to attend her funeral, but he still has three more weeks left of his program before he comes to the club. The guys back home are itching for a new prospect. They want someone to bitch around and have to do their grunt work.

Armor's out doing God knows what, or God knows who. Meanwhile, I've been walking around with Mabel in the local town. It's fifteen miles away from where Chains grew up, and that's where we've been staying. His mother had a massive house back in the sticks, but it sucks when you're craving a Butterfinger and have to drive thirty minutes to get to the nearest gas station.

Mabel and I went out to lunch in town. It wasn't anything special, but I haven't had good pit beef in a really long time. When I saw a fundraiser at the local church, I had to stop and get my girl and me some food. There's nothing better than a hot pit beef sandwich in my eyes. I loaded it up with malt vinegar, onions, ketchup, and mustard. Mabel looked at me like she thought it was going to be the worst thing she'd ever eaten, but when she took a bite, her eyes practically rolled back in her head.

Mabel and I are walking down the street when the familiar rumbling of a bike comes up behind us. I turn, as does she, and we spot not only Chains but someone else on a bike. The guy has blond hair just like Chains does but looks significantly younger. I'd say he's in his early twenties, possibly mid-twenties. Chains and the man bring their bikes over next to the sidewalk and shut them off, making sure they're out of traffic.

"Ops, Mabel, this is my younger brother, Archer." Chains introduces his younger brother, and we give a nod in acknowledgment.

"Nice to meet you, man," I say to him, extending a hand. Archer grabs it and nods.

"It's a pleasure, but with unfortunate circumstances," Mabel tells him, and he nods.

"The circumstances do suck, but she's better off this way. Our mother hadn't been herself in a really long time," Archer tells the group of us, and I notice the way his eyes darken. Not in a physical sense, but in a mental one. Just because she was sick doesn't make losing her any easier, of that, I'm sure.

"Did the doctor let you out early?" Mabel asks, trying to change the subject.

"Something like that. I finished the program as of today, and I was going to stay longer . . . but Chains told me that I have a pretty solid setup back in L.A., so I wanted to give it a go. He said one of the old timers is sober, so that'll help me a bit," Archer speaks up, looking to his brother and then to me.

"Yeah, he's our president's father, Ice. He's opinionated as fuck, so much so that sometimes you're gonna wanna kill him, but he's good people," I explain, getting a laugh from Archer.

"Cool. I think it'll be good for me there. Out here, there's not much to do except drugs and alcohol."

"The club will keep you busy. There's always something to be done," Mabel adds in.

"Yeah, I've heard stories. Apparently, all I'm doing is signing up to be the club's bitch."

"For now. Once you prove yourself to the club, you'll earn your place as a fully patched brother. It all takes time, Archer. Nothing ever happens quickly," Chains tells him.

"And if it does, it's hardly ever worth it," I chime in, and Chains nods.

"Anyway, we're gonna get going. My uncle came into town, and he's up at the hotel. Archer and I are going to spend some time with him. We'll meet you back at the house later," Chains says, and we wave our good-byes. Archer and Chains start their engines and roll up the road. Meanwhile, I wrap my arm around my woman.

"I'm glad you came out with me, out here, I mean."

Mabel turns her head and looks up at me. "Me too. The circumstances are sad, of course, but it's been fun to be on the back of the bike with you. I like it a lot."

I chuckle lightly because my mind goes straight to how many naughty things I could do to her on the back of my bike. "Good, baby, 'cause you're not goin' anywhere. You're my ride or die, my ol' lady for life, and I love you. Fuck, I love how supportive you are of the lifestyle and that you get along with everyone at the club. It's awesome. You're better than any woman I imagined being with. You've surpassed my wildest dreams, baby. I don't think I say that enough."

Mabel's lips shift into a fully heartfelt smile, and she stops, puts her hands around my neck, and kisses me softly. This is what I want. It's what I've always wanted, and I'm never going to take it for granted.

Deathstalkers MC

Stonewall Dynasty

Pins & Needles: Moscow

If you're not already following me, check me out on the
following!

Facebook
Facebook Reader's Group
Goodreads
Bookbub
Amazon
Instagram
Tiktok

MORE FROM THE SATAN'S RAIDERS MC

Armor's Mistake

Fury's Torment